THE
Edge
OF
Paradise

Ken Anderson

A JAN DENNIS BOOK

THOMAS NELSON PUBLISHERS
Nashville • Atlanta • London • Vancouver

Published in Nashville, Tennessee, by Thomas Nelson, Inc., Publishers, and distributed in Canada by Word Communications, Ltd., Richmond, British Columbia.

Unless otherwise noted, Scripture quotations are from the NEW INTERNATIONAL VERSION. Copyright © 1978 by the New York International Bible Society. Used by permission of Zondervan Bible Publishers.

Scripture quotations noted KJV are from the KING JAMES VERSION of the Bible. Scripture quotations noted NKJV are from the NEW KING JAMES VERSION of the Bible, Copyright © 1979, 1980, 1982, Thomas Nelson, Inc., Publishers.

Library of Congress Cataloging-in-Publication Data

Anderson, Ken, 1917-
    The edge of paradise / Ken Anderson.
        p.   cm.
    ISBN 0-7852-8198-3
    1. Near-death experiences—Religious aspects—Fiction. 2. Heart—Diseases—Patients—Fiction. 3. Heaven—Fiction. I. Title.
PS3551.N374E34   1995
813'.54—dc20   94-33180
                                                              CIP

3 4 5 6 7 8 9 10 11 - 00 99 98 97 96

THE
Edge
OF
Paradise

Dedication

To Mrs. A

In musings one day
From a vantage terrestrial,
My thoughts winged away
To surmisings celestial.

I heard no wise word
Of dogma, theology.
No cult was inferred,
No new eschatology.

For naught did I see
But my earthly abiding,
Nor thought I to be
With some seer confiding.

Fret not then, nor fume,
Nor submit me to lecture.
I do not assume.
I only conjecture.

ka

 _____ One

eaven," the Voice cried out, "is the infinite amplification of Earth's sublimest moment!"

The silken Voice, cultured like a woman's but also virile and masculine, seemed distant, like a faraway shout, yet near, like a whisper intended only for me.

"Please repeat," I said.

But the ensuing silence was so intense I wondered if I had heard anything at all. Indeed, as I would eventually learn, the Voice may have been somehow inside me—an interflow of concept and inquiry. I found myself encased in an alien blur, frozen within a transparent substance. For a moment I was afraid. Then, as I reached out to free myself, my arms and my hands moved with an easy grace. And touched nothing!

Similarly, moving my feet, I seemed somehow suspended in a boundless vacuum. Yet securely situated.

"You appear to be a fine candidate," the Voice spoke again. "Your circumstances—you yourself mortal, these surroundings—will cause you to react and inquire in a manner quite unlike what commonly occurs here. That is excellent!"

"I do not understand."

"Of course not! What you observe and experience will help you see the gulf between the most of the temporal and the least of the eternal, better preparing you for your mission!"

I had no idea what the Voice was talking about.

Perhaps, I reasoned, I could make some headway understanding my situation if I reviewed how I'd come to be in such a state.

I remembered rapid acceleration and upward, or perhaps outward, thrust. Anticipation prevailed more than fear while, at the same time, I was filled with deep unfulfillment. This feeling of unfulfillment would come to be the key to my experience.

Recalling further, I remembered a workplace where I stood looking at a desk piled high with uncompleted tasks. A telephone rang.

I remembered a dagger-thrust of pain. Only for a moment, pain, then sudden release.

Then this place.

I remembered nothing more, and I wondered if perhaps the unfulfillment numbed my memory.

"Precisely!" exclaimed the Voice. "Unfulfillment qualifies you for your special mission!"

"My mission?"

"You have been granted unprecedented opportunity and responsibility. You are in limited transcendence."

"Transcendence?"

"Not transcendence!" the Voice reprimanded. "Limited transcendence! You have yet to fully escape mortality. But so it must be for you to perform your mission."

"Have I died?" I asked.

"Death has no function here. It exists outside this realm. Were it not for these special circumstances, the word death would be absent from your vocabulary."

"What are *these* circumstances?"

"Let me tell you first what they are not. Those whom you shall meet here have experienced—that is, are experiencing—full transcendence."

"Which I am not?"

"Not yet."

"But shall?"

"Yes. Now, however, your state is one of rare and limited privilege."

"How might I describe my present state?"

"Such description belongs to the realm from which you have emerged and to which you will return but does not exist in the vocabulary here."

"If my state cannot be described, can it perhaps be defined?" I asked. "What is the definition of limited transcendence?"

"To be mortal among the immortals!"

Before I could question further, I entered—or, more accurately, found myself surrounded by—a place of such compelling beauty I had to shield my eyes. Such splendor exceeded my limited human imagining, and consequently, I could find no words to express what I saw.

I beheld both the dazzling presence and the total absence of any light source, such as the sun or a lamp. Whatever I looked upon radiated its own brightness. Light did not emanate from the objects I beheld, but rather, everything was inherently bright.

I saw what seemed like trees, huge in girth and height, intricate in design and detail. Living gems—flowers for want of a better term—became my carpet and canopy. They bloomed in a thousand colors. I drew fragrances into my depths, yet had no need for breath; I delighted in the total spectrum of color, but had no need for sight. Creatures—birdlike and angelic—darted through the trees and danced among the blossoms. Gourmet tastes erupted upon my tongue although I neither consumed food nor opened my mouth.

Clouds billowed above me, set afire with ten million hues—aurora and mirage, sunrises and sunsets, rainbows glorious to behold.

The infinite amplification of Earth's sublimest moment!

While I experienced an embracing warmth of intimacy, my surroundings extended into an endless reach of horizons: within each other, adjacent to each other, beyond each other. Each was more wide and wondrous than the one before, the farthest intimately near and the nearest immeasurably far.

And then music!

Ten thousand audible fingers caressed my flesh, reaching to enhance my spirit. Symphonies. Chorales. In thundering crescendo, gentle andante, brisk rhythm, and soothing lullaby.

"You view only the onset," said the Voice. "You hear only a prelude."

Though overwhelmed with wonder, I managed to ask, "There are sights and sounds greater than these?"

"What you felt," said the Voice, "is but echo and shadow to those who are in full transcendence. You have experienced a small sampling of the joy of creation: immortal ecstasy reduced to your limited capacity. It is the beauty First Man denied to all when he disobeyed the Sovereign One. Do you understand?"

"I am trying to understand!" I exclaimed with intense effort.

"You shall understand, and when you do, you will realize how much the earthly life offers and how little you mortals use what the Sovereign One has provided for your preparation and orientation."

"Preparation?" I asked. "Orientation?"

"Each in its appointed time," the Voice replied.

"And the . . . the mission of which you speak?"

"You will know what your mission is to be."

New horizons spread out before me, configurations of form and color vast in wonder and detail. I grew numb from the onslaught of it all. It was at once bliss and invigoration. I supposed myself at that moment secure in the ultimate glory to which mortals aspire. Yet when I thought to rest in this abounding state, a pall of remorse came over me. I knew full well I was viewing that which was not mine to possess.

I began weeping and laughing, experiencing both anticipation and anxiety. Was I truly in Heaven? If so, where were the saints and angels? Or was this a cloistered segment of immortality, an outer periphery for those alien to the Divine Realm?

The edge of Paradise, perhaps?

In that moment, of course, I neither knew nor realized that, had my questions been answered, those answers would have been of no significance!

As the visualization about me intensified, I could hear what sounded like the relentless beating of surf. Vaguely at first, then distinctly, the sound became articulate, voicing the words:

> The Spirit searches all things, even the deep things of God. For who among men knows the thoughts of a man except the man's spirit within him? In the same way no one knows the thoughts of God except the Spirit of God. We have not received the spirit of the world but the Spirit who is from God, that we may understand what God has freely given us.

 **Two**

Not weariness. Not sleep. A disturbed repose.

"For those who are ill-prepared at the conclusion of their mortality, transcendence offers little more than disturbed repose. They know, but only scarcely, the Sovereign One's promise of *rest for the people of God.*"

A new voice had spoken.

Turning, I saw a visible form approaching, a body like mine yet, I recognized at once, possessing transcendent qualities. The gender of the visitor was of no importance to me. I shall use the masculine pronoun as a matter of convenience and since I happen to be male.

He looked at me for a long and silent moment. I took special note of his eyes for, in my mortal state, I had always admired people of compassion. This man's eyes radiated such caring that, very quickly, my apprehension ceased.

"You look like someone important," I blurted, much as one would do on Earth when at a loss for words but pressed upon to make an introductory statement.

"Someone important?" he asked. "Ah, yes, I recall

now! An expression from the old vocabulary. Earth language, never used, becomes difficult for the tongue and the ear, does it not?"

"I was not trying to offend you," I managed to say.

"Your words did not offend me. They saddened me. Not since mortality have I met someone whose first observation is temporal. How bound by the fetters of mortality you appear! So also was I! May the Sovereign One enable me to help you in your great need!"

I very nearly took offense, since one of my mortal failings was an aversion to criticism and correction.

"Did you ever compliment someone's shadow?" the stranger asked. "One in full transcendence could observe more of me in my shadow than what you behold and think comely."

"I ask your pardon," I curtly responded.

"No need," he said with contrasting pleasantness. "Actually, my last years on Earth were debilitating. And, before that, I was quite ordinary looking."

"I see you now in the glory of your transcendence?" I asked.

To which my new acquaintance replied, "You see only as much as your limited transcendence allows you to see."

He extended his hand. We shook in a conventional manner, yet did not touch. It also occurred to me, we had not been conversing in the Earth mode of speaking and listening but, rather, communicated without audible speech.

"You prefer conventional speech?" he asked. His lips

moved. His words synchronized with their movement. But his voice had a discordant texture. He continued, his lips not moving, "Or do you like this better?"

"The second way," I responded, aware my own lips had remained firmly set.

"Relax, my friend. What is new in transcendence can never become commonplace but may become customary. So it is, I presume, in your limited state."

Earth's sublimest moment!

"You may call me Procrastin."

"Procrastin," I repeated.

"So named for your own better understanding, since I spent nearly all my earthly life without preparing for transcendence, without properly seeking to be rid of the unfulfillment you now experience." Sadness gave added meaning to his words. "Like so many mortals, like most, I neglected the two provisions by which such preparation, and such riddance, may occur."

"What are those provisions?" I asked.

"The mind and the senses," he replied. "Mortals have limited measures of breath but limitless capabilities for thought and purpose. The dimensions of all mortal brains, as compared to the capabilities of all mortal bodies, show that the mind is meant to envision larger realities than can be experienced within the limitations of mortality. It is sheer folly to use the brain solely or primarily for temporal invention and discernment!"

He turned from me, looking so intently I also turned to see what object held his gaze. I saw nothing. But his next statements became the pivotal concepts illuminating my experiences in limited transcendence.

"The mortal brain," he continued, slowly turning back to me, "was designed for the primary purpose of communing with the Sovereign One! Otherwise, it functions amiss!"

Procrastin's voice, momentarily increased in intensity, now fell to a whisper as he told me, "The human brain has the capacity to contemplate the infinite!"

He hesitated, I assumed for the purpose of giving me time to ponder his words.

"Astrophon will help you understand that the potential of the mortal brain exceeds that of any other temporal entity. For now, let me tell you that, in neglecting my own mind, I inevitably neglected my senses."

"Your five senses?" I asked.

"Oh," he answered, "like most mortals, I indulged the five primary senses. In so doing, I neglected the sixth sense and, consequently, denied myself awareness of the seventh."

"The sixth sense?" I asked, perplexed. "The seventh?"

"You are aware of the five mortal senses?"

"Sight, hearing, touch, taste, and smell," I recited, like a schoolboy.

I thought of the wonders I had encountered in this place, the sounds and sights, tastes and fragrances. I might have spoken further were it not for a loud voice speaking the words that accompanied my entrance into limited transcendence.

Heaven is the infinite amplification of Earth's sublimest moment! Had my new acquaintance spoken? Had I? Might it have been the Voice again? In retrospect I surmised it to have been neither—instead, the statement occurred more audibly or forcefully than would be possible through either speech or hearing. That is to say, the words came to me by virtue of their relevance to my need and circumstances.

"During your own mortality," I asked, "did you find the five senses to be primarily agents of evil?"

"Cancers they can be," Procrastin said softly, "blinding the soul, binding the flesh, enticing the scant years of mortality away from their eternal purpose. Whatever the capabilities of his mind, a mortal—by gratifying the five senses—limits himself to meager thoughts, conduct, and assessments. Fulfillment can never be found in the limited dimensions of the five basic senses! Never! *Your body is a temple of the Holy Spirit,* the Guidebook admonishes. Your body is also the mechanism of the five basic senses."

"Please tell me about the two senses beyond the basic five," I said.

"It is abnormal to isolate the basic five!" Procrastin reprimanded. "We identify the senses correctly only when including all seven! They are inseparable, and to segment the sixth and the seventh is more debilitating than to be deaf and blind and without taste or passion!"

"Seven is the number of perfection," I said, endeavoring to make conversation on a subject for which I had no knowledge.

"Seven is the number of fulfillment!" Procrastin corrected. "The first five senses, while they relate to immortality, are meant to be disciplines by which the two most important senses are experienced. Further, you must understand that only through the seventh sense may one comprehend and love the Sovereign One to the extent of a mortal's capability."

I experienced a new wonder. Words leaped from my mind and became as flashing neon before me. I closed my eyes only to have the visualization so increase in brilliance I opened my eyes once more to shelter them against the intensity.

There are seven senses! Seven is the number of fulfillment!

"Tell me," I at last managed to say, "about the two additional senses."

"Not additional!" Procrastin scolded. "Inclusive!"

His voice mellowed. "The Sovereign One has given to all mortals the sixth sense, the consciousness of His existence."

"I have that sense!" I exclaimed.

"The proudest, most erudite of mortals have it, as do the humble and unlearned."

"And the seventh?" I asked.

Procrastin's eyes abruptly brimmed with tears. He looked at me long and intently, whether as judge or advocate I could not determine.

"Neglect the sixth sense, or pursue it improperly," he

said, "and no mortal can be so much as aware of the seventh sense."

Tears coursed down his cheeks.

"Earth has no greater folly," he lamented, "than to deny one's awareness of the seventh sense!"

> Delight yourself in the LORD and he will give you the desires of your heart.

Had I spoken the words from the Guidebook? Had they surfaced in my mind from my limited reading of the sacred volume? Or were they remembered from an exhortation in the Earth place where I habitually assembled with others on First Day?

"Do you understand the Guidebook's meaning?" Procrastin asked, as he regained control of his emotions. "Those who live in the subordinate senses suppose the promise implies one's sensual desires will be granted. Not so! It is not the mortal's desires which are promised but desires the Sovereign One seeks to implant in the heart of any mortal who wishes to glorify Him! Through those desires, born in the heart of the Sovereign One, comes realization—as well as actualization—of the seventh sense!"

> You will seek me and find me when you seek me with all your heart.

The sixth sense!

> So whether you eat or drink or whatever you do, do it all for the glory of God.

The seventh!

How glibly I had heard those words from the Guidebook at First Day convenings! How lucid and meaningful they were to me now!

"Most mortals make no effort to acquire the seventh sense," I said.

"Although most do not," Procrastin responded, "everyone who chooses may! It is the primary purpose of mortality! While on Earth, I squandered my years in earning a living. I did well. I enjoyed abundance in Earth's goods. I achieved—what is the mortal designation?—ah, yes, a comfortable retirement."

"Such has been my motive," I admitted.

"The word *retirement* belongs only in the vocabulary of dullards, not in those who devote their mortality to serving as fellow workers with the Sovereign One!

"During the third year of my retirement I fell victim to terminal illness. By costly and painful application of geriatric therapy, I managed a full decade of additional mortality."

He no longer wept. His face showed deep pain, a pain unrelated to his former physical ailment, pertaining instead to the distress of a penitent soul.

"Such a fool I had been," he continued, "fearing mortal death instead of anticipating eternal life!

"One of the Earth shepherds came to my aid. With the Guidebook, he helped calm my fretful spirit and led me to the pardon and cleansing which, in one moment, exceeded all the tawdry accomplishments and pleasures of my squandered mortality."

"You discovered the seventh sense?" I asked.

"I had little time to discover, much less do. But I

learned enough to understand its meaning. The seventh sense," he said, "consists of capacity and discernment the Sovereign One alone can bestow. In essence, the seventh sense is comprehension and practice whereby mortality is seen as a massive and diminishing negative, unless, as when linked to the eternal, mortality becomes the diligent preparation for transcendence!

"Theologus and Algoris, whom you will meet, can explain more fully. I, you will remember, had so little time to explore the seventh sense, much less pursue it."

"Will they also explain to me the mission I am to perform?" I asked. But Procrastin had gone, leaving me alone.

From the Guidebook, I heard:

> No eye has seen, no ear has heard, no mind has conceived what God has prepared for those who love Him.

Three

Can Earth's sublimest moment be experienced within the five primary senses?" I asked, forgetting for the moment that I stood alone.

"Every mortal, whatever his Earth circumstance, encounters what becomes his own sublimest moment." It was once again the Voice—pleasant, like conversation with a friend at tea. "Albeit, the sublimest moment attainable in mortality, though related to the primary senses, can be perceived solely in the context of the seventh sense."

"Within the seventh sense, or by means of the seventh sense?"

"The five primary senses rise to their fullest enhancement only through the seventh sense," was the reply. "The seven senses are meant to be a totality."

"So then," I said, "the ultimate experience of Earth's sublimest moment in itself relates to the seventh sense."

"Most assuredly! But only if one implements this sense!"

I pondered a moment, then asked, "In the search for the seventh sense, ought mortals to subdue the five primary senses?"

"Have you in this one moment forgotten?" the Voice reproved.

"You do not segment the seven senses. They are a totality!"

"Let me state my question this way. In correct priority, mortals ought to seek the seventh sense rather than Earth's sublimest moment."

"You must more carefully guard your thinking. You persist in envisioning Earth's sublimest moment as a measure of the five primary senses. Sentium, whom you shall meet, will help you realize how far, indeed, the seventh sense transcends the mere quest for gratifying experiences of mortal flesh."

"I am confused," I protested. "Since the seventh sense is of such importance to mortals, why are so many denied the knowledge of its existence?"

From the Guidebook came the remembered words, *Small is the gate and narrow the road that leads to life, and only a few find it.*

"One of the foremost detriments of First Man's fall was the broken lineage of inquiry," the Voice continued.

"Lineage?" I asked. "Inquiry?"

"What is the primary attribute of a child's initial conversations?"

"The asking of questions," I replied.

"An endowment of the Sovereign One!" exclaimed the Voice. "Those who believe in the chance appearance of mortals upon Earth are hard pressed to explain how it is that every child is born with the necessary curiosity to inquire about the Sovereign One and His doings. Families, therefore, are meant to be nests of nurtured inquiry. The Guidebook abounds in responses to the questions of children. Questions left unanswered, however, or given erroneous response, cause a child's gift for inquiry to quickly deteriorate into mere desire for material knowledge. It was not so intended by the Sovereign One."

More words from the Guidebook came to my thoughts. *If any of you lacks wisdom, he should ask God, who gives generously to all.*

"The Guidebook abounds with such promises," said the Voice.

> So do not worry, saying, "What shall we eat?" or "What shall we drink?" or "What shall we wear?" For the pagans run after all these things, and your heavenly Father knows that you need them. But seek first His kingdom and His righteousness, and all these things will be given to you as well.

Food . . . drink . . . The five senses!
His kingdom and His righteousness. The seventh sense!

> Trust in the LORD with all your heart and lean not on your own understanding; in all your

ways acknowledge Him, and He will make
your paths straight.

"There are multitudes more," said the Voice sternly.
"Were you a more motivated student of the Guidebook,
such promises would saturate your mind."

"But I did read the Guidebook," I defended. Then,
thinking more wisely, I asked, "Is it possible to read the
Guidebook, to also study it, and yet not experience the
seventh sense?"

"A common failing with mortals. Theologus will
instruct and warn you of those who pursue the teachings
of the Guidebook in their own vanity. For now, be aware
the Guidebook can only be properly understood either
when seeking the seventh sense or when nurturing the
seventh sense."

I remembered what Procrastin had said about the
brain.

"Ah, yes," exclaimed the Voice, "the mortal brain!"

"Intended to identify and implement the seven
senses," I said.

"Spoken as though you were in the beginning of full
transcendence!" the Voice commended. "What a fine
candidate you truly are!"

My normal reaction to such commendation would be
pride. Instead, a fountain-thrust of gratitude welled up
from my innermost.

Gratitude and expectation!

Suddenly, a glorious thing happened. Hosts of voices
surrounded me, not a Babel of confusion, however, but

an audible montage of inspiring eloquence. Prophets and sages, whose words had been eternalized in the Guidebook, addressed me with the wonder and zest which had been theirs as the Sovereign One first communicated through them.

> When Your words came, I ate them; they were my joy and my heart's delight, for I bear Your name, O LORD God Almighty.

> Your word is a lamp to my feet and a light for my path.

> I will instruct you and teach you in the way you should go; I will counsel you and watch over you.

> Do not let this Book of the Law depart from your mouth; meditate on it day and night, so that you may be careful to do everything written in it. Then you will be prosperous and successful.

On and on flowed the words—exhorting, comforting, assuring—until my spirit seemed to break free from my body and become, in itself, a proclamation of promise and praise!

Then the audible montage ceased. More accurately, mere words faded from hearing. In their stead, I became immersed in sublime contemplation. The essence of truth came upon me like a benediction.

"There is no need for words!" I cried out.

"None whatever," replied the Voice. "Mortal speech is the sound of weakness more than the utterance of strength. Speech was bestowed for the primary purpose of enabling mortals to cry out to the Sovereign One and, finding Him, to share their discovery with others."

My thoughts submerged deeper and deeper into this splendid abyss of contemplation. Two words from Earth vocabulary remained to enrich my joyous abstraction: questions, answers.

Thesis and antithesis they became, point and counterpoint, the content in which fulfillment spawns and becomes reality.

"Awareness!" spoke the Voice, bringing my reverie to abrupt conclusion.

"As I was just then," I said, disappointed, "I could wish to remain forever."

"You were experiencing but the first dimension of awareness."

"Awareness lies beyond questions and answers?"

"Precisely!" replied the Voice. "It is in awareness that those in full transcendence become liberated from the need for questions and answers. You might say mortality is the question, immortality the answer. To question is mortal, to know immortal."

"All knowledge is known in transcendence?" I asked.

"Again, and expectedly, you speak from the vantage and measurement of mortality. No such dimensions as 'all' or 'part' exist here. Full transcendence is to know and to be always knowing, to discover and to be always discovering."

"The unanswered questions of Earth are answered here?"

"How hindered you are by the trivia of mortality," the Voice chided.

As before, I took offense.

"Affrontation is solely an Earth experience," said the Voice. To this he added, "I am aware of your questions. First, however, let me ask you. Do you recall the words of the Guidebook? *'No one can lay any foundation other than the one already laid.'*"

"I remember," I said, adding, "*'If any man builds on this foundation using gold, silver, costly stones, wood, hay or straw, his work will be shown for what it is.'*"

The clarity of those words overwhelmed me!

"*Wood, hay or straw* relates to the five senses," I said. "*Gold, silver, costly stones* relates to the seventh sense!"

In the wake of my own words, I stood at a vantage point overlooking a typical Earth community.

On the streets, in homes, at schools, churches, places of business and amusement, I watched mortals live out their years, generation after generation in time lapse.

I saw the poor at sparse tables, the affluent in banquet halls. I observed people in marketplaces hawking their wares, counting their proceeds. I observed artisans at work. I listened as the learned dispensed space/time knowledge.

I watched those of little faith like me hurry to their

First Day sanctuaries, sit for a restless hour, and scamper away to continue the pandering of their primary senses.

Young maidens, unconvinced by either instruction or example to guard the blush of virtue, flaunted their comely graces before young and leering eyes. Male and female—breathless, passions aflame—sought out dark places in which to rendezvous. Old men looked on in envy, their aging bodies unable to satiate their minds yet full with libertine recollections.

"Early on they left behind their childhood legacy of questioning," said the Voice. "They are capable of glory; they bring upon themselves, in its place, ignominy."

"*Wood, hay or straw*!" I cried out in tears. To this I added, "Tell me! Please, tell me! Must they burn in eternal fire? Must they?"

"Your persistence shall not be ignored," said the Voice.

"And my mission?"

"When you are prepared, you shall know and understand."

For the first time, I realized that those questions, which had plagued me for so much of my Earth existence, remained in my mind but were, at times such as this interim with the Voice, diminished in importance.

And then, from the Guidebook:

> What is your life? You are a mist that appears for a little while and then vanishes.

 **Four** _____

In a manner to which I was becoming accustomed, I entered new surroundings, perceiving those altered acoustics one detects when moving from a hard surface into a draped and carpeted room. Although encompassed by intense silence, I became conscious of an emotion related to music. Not of voices, not of instruments, but of the exhilaration in which an audience basks after the orchestra has played its final encore and the conductor no longer responds to applause.

"Pleasant, isn't it?"

Beside me, as though we had been companions for some time, appeared an individual I initially assessed as an old man.

"A multitude of pardons!" he exclaimed. "I was so enraptured by a delightful thought I presumed you to be one of my usual associates. Let me introduce myself."

"You are Astrophon," I said, both surprised and pleased at my perceptiveness.

"I am Astrophon," he affirmed. He gave no apparent

notice of my having identified him without prior introduction.

I took closer note of my new acquaintance. Though he had, as I said, the appearance one associates with advanced years, he was buoyant. He had more the zest of a college freshman than the sagacity of a hoary-yeared academic.

"I assume your name holds special significance here," I said.

"As in the case of Procrastin, my name is a convenience for your limited transcendence."

He spread his arms with the solemnity of one at worship. The gesture—like the opening of huge curtains—revealed a vast spectacle. Had it not been for my earlier view of horizons, I would surely have covered my eyes.

Provisionally liberated from perspectives and dimensions of my past, I saw the magnitude of space as though it were some animated and immense diorama. Entire galaxies, whirling and intertwining, vaulted to immeasurable heights above me, plummeted aeons of light-years below.

There was both intimacy and extent. It was as though I could reach out with one hand and touch the Star of the North, extend the other to the Cross of the South, and yet look out upon infinite distances.

The constellation known as Pegasus winged past me in the cosmic expanse. Orion stalked his prey. Cepheus sat upon his imagined throne.

During my student years, I had charted the position

of Andromeda as the farthest known point in space. Now the constellation, with its bright star Alpheratz a ball of fire before my eyes, came within reach like flowers in a garden.

"Do I view the actual heavens," I asked, "or a diorama?"

Astrophon became amused. "Does it matter?" he asked, quickly adding, "What you see is really beyond reality. That is to say, beyond time. Let me show you."

I stood, so it seemed, yet was transported on into the heavens—beyond Alpheratz, beyond the farthest glimmer of remote Andromeda—until we looked out upon a display of gem-like celestial bodies.

"This is the constellation Quandorix, so named by the Sovereign One because of His great joy in fashioning it. I knew nothing of its existence during my mortality. Nor shall any mortal. For the last light of Quandorix reached Earth aeons before the creation of First Man."

"Quandorix is extinct?"

"As are many other wonders of the heavens."

"Then we have gone backward in time to view it!" I exclaimed.

"Algoris, whom you shall meet, will familiarize you with the Eternity Hiatus. Then perhaps you will better understand."

We were in the instant returned to our first viewing of the heavens, the magnitude of which struck me more forcefully than before.

"Indescribable!" I exclaimed.

"The whole of what you see," Astrophon corrected,

"comprises less quantity, relatively speaking, than a grain of sand upon Earth!"

"Surely no! It appears vast beyond measurement!"

"Beyond measurement? As Algoris will subsequently explain, that which can be measured or enumerated is temporal. As you know, Earth minds have comprehended the universe to be contained within itself. Space/time, however, can be held as a pebble in the Sovereign One's hand!"

From the Guidebook came the words: *He determines the number of the stars and calls them each by name. Great is our LORD and mighty in power; His understanding has no limit.*

"The heavens are temporal. The stars can be numbered. It is the Sovereign One's *understanding* that is eternal," said Astrophon. "The Sovereign One, eternal and infinite, created the temporal and finite to provide nurture wherein mortals could pursue and enhance immortality. Do you understand?"

"Perhaps I shall," I managed to reply.

"Excellent!" Astrophon exclaimed. "The Sovereign One is pleased!"

"The Sovereign One observes us here?"

"Assuredly! The Sovereign One notes every breath you ever take. He numbers the hairs of your head, the cells of your body. No temporal event escapes His notice."

"I am unprepared to understand all you are saying."

"Such an admission early in your limited transcendence enhances the potential of your sojourn here!

Mortals are born and mortals die without comprehending as much!"

I waited in silence for him to continue.

"You remember the pyrotechnical celebrations on earth?"

"I do."

"And mortal venturings into space?"

"Yes."

"The farthest thrust of an Earth rocket may be likened to a firework soaring a few hundred feet into the air!" He sighed, then smiled and added, "Man's pretensions amuse the angels!"

After he stopped speaking, we seemed to be projected at the speed of thought. Planets and their moons, sun after sun after sun, nebulae of galactic magnitude afloat in void, all of them wonders looming and becoming distinct and then receding and fading from view.

"Will mortals ever traverse space at this velocity?" I blurted.

Astrophon did not reply.

Was he avoiding me? *Whatever the mind can imagine, the hand can fashion,* I remembered reading.

"Do you believe it so?"

Astrophon's inquiry drew me from my train of thought.

"Let me say," he added, "that the Sovereign One, our Creator, did not mean for mortals to spend their short lives designing methods to escape the terrain provided for their preparation."

"Exploring space is sinful?"

"In itself, such conduct is neutral. Whatever aids a mortal's preparation is good. Whatever hinders a mortal's preparation is evil. You must understand, for the success of your mission, that all mortals are imprisoned in space/time. But only in a sense, as you shall learn. The hand of mortals is weak but the mind of mortals is capable of reducing space/time to the girth of a grain of sand."

"Is space/time finite?" I asked.

"Lips like yours, remember, have declared the universe to be contained within itself," Astrophon replied. "That which can be measured or enumerated is temporal. You recall the thesis of your limited transcendence?"

"*Heaven*," I responded, "*is the infinite amplification of Earth's sublimest moment.* Is that thesis adequate?"

"A commendable question! Your perception indicates how inclined you are for limited transcendence! When you finally come into full transcendence you will realize how meagerly your thesis expresses the difference between mortality and immortality. Yet even during mortality, you must remember, much of what you are perceiving here could have been previously learned."

"How?" I asked loudly, for his statement had startled me.

"From the Guidebook!" His words had the sting of reprimand.

I thought with shame of the scant time I had ever given to the volume!

"That which is most to mortals is least to immortals," continued Astrophon. "As stated in the Guidebook, *The heavens declare the glory of God.* To be sure. But how impoverished are those who look for the ultimate within the finite, who note not that, as the Guidebook states, *no eye has seen, no ear has heard, no mind has conceived what God has prepared for those who love Him!*"

How wrong I had been! How very wrong!

"It is in the five senses," I said, "by which men search the heavens to seek that which can be found only in the sixth and seventh senses."

"Found only in the sixth and seventh when those senses are first used to search the Guidebook in preparation for transcendence!" Astrophon corrected. "Come," he continued, gesturing.

We each took a step and came the same moment to a laboratory. In the center of this laboratory stood a large scientific instrument. Astrophon stepped to the instrument, pointed to dual eyepieces and beckoned me. I came and placed my eyes against the viewing device.

"I call this my dimensiotron," he said.

He spoke and I beheld stereoptic wonders as arresting as my previous view of the heavens.

I turned to Astrophon to ask, "Is the instrument focused on deeper reaches of outer space than what I have seen before?"

He gestured for me to resume looking, which I did, and then he said, "You are not looking into outer space. You are examining the inner dimensions of an atom."

"Inner?" I gasped, stepping aside. "An atom?"

Astrophon touched my shoulder, guiding me back to

the eyepieces. "I will instruct the instrument to split the atom for you," he said.

As I watched, a nuclear detonation took place, soundless and without percussion, yet broader than the sky, more outreaching than my remembrance of Andromeda. It lasted for but a moment and was followed by a new and more entrancing display.

"You see one-half of the atom," Astrophon said.

"But it is larger and more beautiful than before," I told him.

"Most surely? Indeed? And now the instrument will split the half you are viewing!"

There came another explosion, introducing visual drama of compounding wonder.

"I do it again!" exclaimed Astrophon, for all his erudite bearing becoming as enthusiastic as a child. "Again! Again! Again!"

Explosion after explosion, wonder upon wonder before my eyes!

Astrophon explained that the two eyepieces view separate phenomena: inner space on my right, outer space on the left. I watched in awe until I could scarcely detect which was the inner atom, which the vault of space, for the two became as one and my view became unified vastness!

At last I turned from the instrument, covering my eyes.

"Space I can accept!" I cried out, weeping and laughing, shouting and whispering. "But the atom astounds me! Can one split the atom endlessly?"

"What you have seen is less than a grain of sand, remember, for that which is most to mortals is least to immortals."

"But if you can go on, endlessly, splitting the halves of what you have severed before, then—" I paused. "Cannot the half of a previous quantity be itself cut into two parts?" I pointed to the dual eyepieces. "Is there then infinity in both directions, up and down?"

"You cannot apply finite pragmatism to infinite phenomena. To divide half into half, and half into half, continuing the process endlessly, would necessitate transforming the finite into the infinite, and that is forever impossible. Have you so soon forgotten? That which can be measured or enumerated is temporal. The Sovereign One, remember also, can hold it all in the palm of His hand!"

"But . . ."

I could say no more.

No eye has seen, no ear has heard, no mind has conceived what God has prepared for those who love Him.

"Procrastin told you of the seventh sense," Astrophon said, "and you are grasping that often-neglected reality. Do remember, however, that the seventh sense is solely an Earth experience."

I had not thought of this.

"Space/time is the Sovereign One's statement to the finite mind. As Algoris will more fully explain, mortals too often see space/time as the ultimate rather than the immediate. Mortals should contemplate the snowflake before they contemplate the stars. The obsession that he and his present reality are greater than they are too often impels a mortal to explore space/time. It is not awe of the Sovereign One but a distorted view of reality itself.

"In my Earth experience, I participated in the dispatch of space probes. Planet to planet, moon to moon, I reviewed the findings in awe and anticipation. I saw Earth increasingly as a lesser element in space, not realizing how in character it was for the Sovereign One to center His attention upon one small planet, even as He can concentrate on one mortal, number every hair of your head, separately fashion each snowflake, design one atom with wonder. Algoris will more fully explain the Sovereign One's mathematics."

"Contemplate the snowflake before the stars," I said quietly.

"And yourself before Andromeda," Astrophon added.

He gestured for us to move on and, in that instant, we stood within what I first assumed to be a cathedral.

"I often come to this library," Astrophon said.

"Library?" I asked. I saw no books.

"Take care not to regress in the progress you are making!"

I understood the rebuke sufficiently to ask, "Transcended libraries have no need for books?"

"Books are temporal. They would be a hindrance here."

It occurred to me that the entire structure, vacant to normal vision, was full with content. Earth books, silent

and dormant until taken and opened, were here sup-
planted by concepts one might find in a research facility
devoted to an exhaustive compilation of data on astron-
omy and the elements and factors of space/time. Like
silent voices, these concepts were all about me, coming
directly to my mind without hearing or reading. Not in
confusion, however, but in an orderly manner, as if a
genius had succeeded in learning all that could be known
of a subject and recollected material as needed.

"How much of mortal knowledge about space/time
is contained here?"

"All that is known and all that is knowable."

"Such knowledge is finite?"

"The Sovereign One can hold space/time—both entity and essence—in the palm of His hand!" Astrophon
rebuked. Then, gently, he added, "Algoris will assist you
with a clearer understanding. Since I came so ill-prepared for transcendence, one of my disciplines has been
to learn how much of what mortals call profound really
is less than elementary."

"Those in fullest transcendence would not come to
this library?"

"No more than a university professor would enroll
in kindergarten!"

"The fullness of truth can only be acquired through
the seventh sense?" I asked.

Astrophon did not respond.

"Please tell me," I continued, "how it is you speak of
being ill-prepared for transcendence?"

Such a degree of sadness swept over Astrophon's face, making him seem like a stranger.

"If I should not ask . . ."

"You have the right to ask, for it is my duty to assist you."

I regretted my inquiry. Such sentiment in transcendence was indeed perplexing!

For several moments he stood immobile, silent. Then, musing more than responding, he said, "Like so many supposedly learned mortals, I gave myself more to the accumulation and the evaluation of data than to the search for truth. When my youth was gone and I realized how quickly one's years pass, I began to look more inquiringly at what I thought to be material reality. Until then I had thought myself too sophisticated to allow any creed to augment or influence my search for truth.

"One evening, after spending several hours in the observatory, I was adjusting controls to an ionization chamber when I became curious about the movement of my fingers. Then, remembering I had promised my wife not to work late, I lifted a sleeve to display my watch. I neglected checking the time when I abruptly realized that the timepiece—like the suns of space, like the flesh of my fingers, like the equipment in the observatory, like the observatory building itself—all consisted of identical atoms!

"Identical, yes, but also inorganic. The stones and stars, the metal, the flesh in my hand! Some living, some lifeless, all identical! In sudden panic, I turned to my sixth sense!"

"And thus the seventh?" I primed.

Seeming not to have heard me, yet responding as if he had, Astrophon said, "Though I once tracked the planets in their orbits, knew the stars by name, I did not have so much as a child's understanding of the seventh sense."

He began to weep.

I also wept.

"*Gold, silver, costly stones,*" he said at last, his voice laboring over each word, "*wood, hay or straw.* I did not then understand, nor did I ever in my mortality attain such knowledge, that the vastness of space/time, as mortals measure, is meant to impress upon us the minuteness of space/time by immortal calculations."

"Am I to understand," I probed with caution, "that you spent no time at all preparing for transcendence?"

"None! Even when I turned to the Sovereign One, it was with reservation. I wanted Him to prove Himself, to define Himself, foolishly unaware that the Sovereign One could only have granted my request by becoming less than Himself."

"Less than Himself?"

"The Sovereign One is the Sovereign One. He is what He is. How else shall we describe or define Him?"

> How precious to me are your thoughts, O
> God! How vast is the sum of them!

"Others come here unprepared?" I asked.

"We do not assess others. I only know that, great

though my joy and fulfillment, I am limited to the outer periphery of celestial knowledge and experience."

"But did not your inquiries as to the Sovereign One's creation help to prepare you?"

"The manner of my search hindered rather than helped. Algoris will assist you to understand."

He turned now and, appearing much like the old man of my initial impression, walked slowly away. I wanted to recall him, to ask what he perhaps knew of my mission.

I refrained.

"Of your encounter with me," I heard him say, "remember it was I who told you one perceives that for which one is prepared."

> What good is it for a man to gain the whole world, yet forfeit his soul?

Whether I heard the words spoken or perceived them in some other manner, I do not recall. I only know they assumed for me, in that moment, a clarity of meaning I would cherish always.

Five

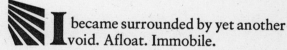I became surrounded by yet another void. Afloat. Immobile.

Conscious in mind and body, with heart and soul anticipant.

A balm of serenity and a continuing mood of disquieting unfulfillment equally came upon me, but I could not then, nor can I now, describe this feeling of incompleteness. It might best be likened to the Earth emotion by which any ecstasy, any pinnacle of accomplishment or pursuit of well-being, tends to have a dispiriting aftermath.

"Is this a foretaste of what immortality will be like for me?" I asked aloud. "Am I even less prepared for transcendence than was Procrastin or Astrophon?"

"The ultimate of mortality is emptiness," I heard the Voice say. "The ultimate of immortality is fulfillment."

"Fulfillment comes only in the seventh sense?"

"Fulfillment comes only through the seventh sense."

I asked further but received no response. However, a

third spokesman approached. In contrast to Astrophon, he appeared to be young and somewhat dashing.

"Algoris?" I asked, pleased once more at my ability to identify a transcendent newcomer.

He gave no response, because—as I now understood—my capability was of no consequence.

"Unfulfillment is a mercy given by the Sovereign One," said Algoris. "As hunger impels animals to search for food, so unfulfillment is meant to guide mortals into recognition of their sixth sense and implementation of their seventh. The Guidebook classifies those temporal pursuits by which mortals wrongly seek satisfaction as *vanity of vanities*. Sentium will further assist you with this."

"You speak of lust, gluttony, and covetousness?" I asked.

Algoris sighed, lightly shaking his head. I felt reproved but was unsure why.

"Such spiritual felonies as lust, gluttony, covetousness, and their like," he explained, "might better be categorized as misdemeanors when compared to those mortal assumptions which defy the Sovereign One's wisdom, authority, and counsel."

"Please clarify."

"An example," he replied, "from my own Earthtime circumstances. Ancients, as you call them, and as I once did, included those who regarded mathematics as the fulfilling science. From their progeny to your contemporaries, this false reckoning has been continually modified but consistently embraced."

With a gesture of his hand, he turned my attention to where we now stood, and I observed a spectacle that reduced prior astonishments to a mere prelude.

I had sometimes imagined what it might be like to enter the memory banks of a computer; now I realized I was there. Instead of the previous near and endless horizons, or the vastness and yet the intimacy of space, now surging electronic impulses surrounded me. These impulses produced, in nanoseconds, an ever-changing array of both simple and complex equations. The equations were in modern Arabic but also Babylonian cuneiform and Egyptian hieratic, Sumerian wedges and Mayan vigesimals. The computer functioned in algorithmic and procedural languages, in simple binary code, and in profound logic.

"I am overwhelmed!" I managed to say.

"Too easily so!" Algoris rebuked. Then, humoring me, he added, "What you see likens not to grains of sand but, rather, a child's counting of one-to-ten. A computer itself is more simple than an abacus, a mere utilization of one for 'yes' and zero for 'no.'"

"You are saying mathematics is finite, that there is a number beyond which there are no more numbers?"

I thought of Astrophon's revelations.

My wonder turned to cowardice, as the numerics took on flesh and breath—like serpents hissing at me, showing their fangs; jurors agreeing upon my condemnation; demons leering and exulting; grotesquely-caricatured people, who—like Procrastin, like Astrophon, like me—had squandered opportunities for fulfillment and preparation.

"What is this?" I cried out.

"Mathematics is irreconcilably in opposition to mortality," Algoris explained.

"It is?" I asked, perplexed by such an assumption.

"It is no assumption," he countered. "Mathematics hint of the infinite but, in actuality, provide the shackles by which space/time imprisons mortals within the finite. Mathematics measures the dimensions of unfulfillment."

"I can't understand that," I said.

"Never mistake inexperience for inability," Algoris comforted. He paused, then added, "Or knowledge for wisdom."

There came now the throaty rumble of electronic thunder. The surrounding numerics became indistinct, although present and active. Then, with pristine clarity, the number seven emerged from every calculation in which it appeared. Sevens struck me, encircled me, penetrated me.

Seven! Seven! Seven!

To myself, I said, "Perhaps the foremost purpose of mathematics is to measure the smallness of mortality."

"So it is!" Algoris seemed pleased. "As you heard from the lips of Astrophon—"

"—what is most to mortals is least to immortals," I broke in.

From somewhere unknown came the words of the Guidebook: *When I consider Your heavens, the work of*

*Your fingers, the moon and the stars, which You have
set in place, what is man that You are mindful of him?*

"*What is man?*" Algoris reiterated. "He is one! Only
and ever one! For, to the Sovereign One, the largest
mathematical equation conceivable becomes paltry
compared to the single unit quantity of each and any one
mortal. One! One! One!"

The bombarding sevens, which had so overwhelmed
me, now gave way to the number one, then intermit-
tently to one and seven.

"One! Seven!" Algoris cried out. "One! Seven! One!
Seven!"

"Does the Sovereign One disdain mathematics?" I
was at last able to inquire.

"It is the unique capacity of omnipotence and om-
niscience to look upon each grain of sand, each hair
of the head, each mortal of Earth, as though none
other existed."

Seven! One! Seven! One!

The visualization intensified until I felt as though I
might perish from the throes of it.

Seven! Seven! Seven!

Like lightning.

One! One! One!

Like thunder.

I either heard or spoke the words: *Heaven is the
infinite amplification of Earth's sublimest moment!*

"It is!" cried Algoris.

"It is," I repeated softly.

"Were mathematics to be, on Earth, a science of

transcendence, which it is not, E=mc^2 would be here a diminutive of one plus one," Algoris said. "Or, more accurately, a diminutive of one equals one."

"Does mathematics have any function in this place?" I asked.

"Mathematics tabulates material data only."

"*What is most to mortals is least to immortals,*" I mused.

We entered a new arena.

"This compartment," Algoris told me, "could be contained within the smallest particle visible to an Earth inhabitant's eyesight. It is a contraption—like a child's toy, really—which I designed for my own amusement but discarded shortly after my transcendence as I came to more fully know and to be known. I selected it just now for your experience.

"A word of caution, however. As we observe, keep in mind that trying to categorize and comprehend the finite makes mortals vulnerable to folly."

"Is it wise to ignore material realities?" I asked.

"Material reality is its own unreality!" Algoris sang out in delight. "The stuff of Earth appears tangible to the five senses. But the stuff of Earth, in the fullness of meaning, is exceedingly unreal."

He gestured to a blank wall, upon which appeared, in large and luminous figures, the equation 1+1=2, changing to 2+2=4, and then 4+4=8, 8+8=16. On and on with ever higher figures, in ever increasing velocity. Addition changed to multiplication, then interspersed sum and product.

Addition upon addition, multiplication upon multiplication, a jumble of disarray, a mass of precision and clarity.

Then, suddenly, all disappeared except for the initial 1+1=2. I sighed with relief. Momentary relief, however, for the 1+1=2 equation disintegrated into millions of fractions, no two of equal value.

"The mathematics of infinity?" I asked.

Algoris laughed. "You are both perceptive and imperceptive!" he said. "How can mathematics enumerate the immeasurable? Must you so quickly forget? That which can be measured or enumerated is temporal! And the temporal is always finite!"

To the Sovereign One, I remembered, the largest and only numeric is one.

"The numeral one, in its fullest essence," Algoris reinforced, "measures infinity as clearly as can be understood by mortals. The essence of it is this. The Sovereign One, who is eternally One, seeks intimacy with each mortal. One seeks one, thereby becoming one!"

He hesitated a moment.

Then he said, "Only the numeral one is positive and valid. All other numerals are fractional and are diminished by mortal attempts to increase them. Do you understand?"

I did not.

"But you do know that each mortal is only one. You know that the Sovereign One, being infinite, desires communion with each mortal as if just one existed, and

He can relate to each and every one exclusive of each and every other one!"

"One!" I cried out. "I am one! The Sovereign One is One! And we are one in Him!"

"And all else is fractional, self-destructive," said Algoris.

He pointed again to the wall. There appeared the equation 1/2 x 1/2 = 1/4. The fractions began to multiply, revealing a simple but engrossing aspect of mathematics.

1/4 x 1/4 = 1/16.

1/16 x 1/16 = 1/256.

1/256 x 1/256 = 1/65,536.

"Do you see it?" Algoris asked. "Do you understand?"

"Multiplication diminishes," I gasped, "when we recognize the number one as the eternal entity! The larger the numbers, the lesser the quantity! Mathematics measures the dimensions of unfulfillment!"

"For," added Algoris, "the fraction is the common denominator of mortality. The pursuit of wealth, the appeasement of desire, the quest for comfort and affluence—all decrease in value with each accumulation. You will learn more of the fractionizers."

"Those preparing for transcendence should spurn Earth's wealth?" I asked.

"Earth has no wealth, only substance. Value consists solely in mortal appraisal of Earth substance. To accumulate Earth substance and think it wealth is like impoverishing one's mind and thinking it wisdom. It is to ignore the fractionizers."

I remembered something called an Eternity Hiatus.

"Yes!" exclaimed Algoris. "The birth of mathematics, one might say, *was* the Eternity Hiatus!"

Waiting for him to continue, I saw that we now stood in a new enclosure. A large dome spread above, like the projection surface of a planetarium. As I looked, this dome descended, becoming smaller until it fit snugly about us.

For a moment, I felt imprisoned.

Then the dome became transparent, or so it seemed, and above it stretched a longitudinal ceiling, or a floor of some sort. I could look to the far end of this surface, to my right or to my left and, at the point of apparent ending, see the area extend farther and farther to no place of termination. It was a spectacle new to my eyes.

"Actually," I heard Algoris say, "I built this at the suggestion of our mutual friend, Astrophon."

"What is it?" I asked.

"A trite visualization of the Eternity Hiatus in which space/time and mathematics and mortality have existed for an era comparable in transcendence to a millisecond. You understand, of course, that so much as a millisecond does not exist here."

I, of course, did not understand.

"Remember the words of the Guidebook?" Algoris continued, "*With the Lord a day is like a thousand years, and a thousand years are like a day.* The statement could as easily have been, 'An aeon is as a millisecond and a millisecond as an aeon.' Or it could have been 'aeons of aeons.'" He gestured to the far-reaching expanse above. "This longitudinal surface represents to me the expanse of eternity—its never-beginning, its never-ending. The enclosure in which we stand represents space/time, the whole of space/time."

He pointed to a specific point above us. I looked and saw a glittering point of light which at first blinded me.

He gestured to the longitudinal surface, saying, "Think of that as the endless expanse of eternity. Measurements do not exist. Time has no relevance. Yet, for our better understanding, we may think of it as a progression of existence."

Once again he focused on the point of light above.

"The Sovereign One is as much Love and Mercy as He is Sovereign and Eternal. He needed terrain in which to give forth this Love and Mercy. Thus he ordained the Eternity Hiatus. He created space/time, the earth, and First Man and all the living beings of the planet. For one millisecond, we may say to better understand, the Sovereign One yielded Himself to time and finite dimensions.

"All of this, the aeons of space/time, the millennia and eras and generations of Earth—all were submitted to the apparent reality of time measurement." He gestured to the area around us. "To mortals, time has distinct duration. To the Sovereign One, even the aeons of existence and inevitable extinction of such wonders as the constellation Quandorix—all took place in the millisecond, in the Eternity Hiatus!" As Algoris concluded, he again pointed to the bright point of light above us. "It is a wonder of the Sovereign One's wisdom—aeons of space/time comprising a mere millisecond of eternity!"

"All the events of our lives occur in a moment," I said. "I am contemporary with the patriarchs!"

Algoris did not respond. He had gone, in the manner of others before him.

I stood alone.

And then, from the pages of the Guidebook, came the words:

> Before the mountains were born or you
> brought forth the earth and the world, from
> everlasting to everlasting you are God.

"O Sovereign One!" I cried.

Six

It is indeed perilous to calculate mortality by numbers or to so measure possessions and attainments."

It was Theologus speaking.

"On each day subsequent to your birth, your mortality diminished, for gestation is the preliminary stage of demise."

"I had not thought of mathematics as a theological subject," I said.

"All of mortality relates to theology!"

"During your own Earth life," I asked, "were you a prolonged student of theology?"

"Throughout my academic and adult years."

I did not immediately note the dismay on the face of my new consultant, and I said with enthusiasm, "Then you must have entered transcendence properly prepared! You can be of much assistance to me!"

Theologus remained silent, and I noted how troubled he had become.

"Theologians are as vulnerable to error as are scientists," he said. "In my case, I dared to attempt the measurement of truth, to categorize mercy and grace as best suited my own intellectual whims, not realizing that mortals cannot measure the attributes of God.

"From the moment First Man and First Woman disobeyed the Sovereign One by endeavoring to expand their capability for knowledge, mathematical assumptions have distorted the mortal search for fulfillment. Disobedience gave origin to the deadliest of the fractionizers—pride, greed, and lust. Mortals ventured outward from identity with the Sovereign One. They dwarfed time and distance by their successive inventions. They built towering monuments to their craft and cunning. They modified the Decalogue and mortalized the Sovereign One. Addition and multiplication became their doctrines, luxury and quantity the measures of their successes.

"What greatness might they attain? Set foot on moons and planets? Maneuver atoms? Increase longevity? Moderate the consequences of iniquity?

"Mortals sought to fathom the mysteries of the material universe. The search concluded not in a secret hidden among the stars, no monstrous compilation but, instead, the simple formula $E=mc^2$! For the secret of material reality lay not beyond the telescope but deep within the microscope! Fractionizers they were! Fractionizers!"

"Why must truth be so elusive?" I asked.

"Elusive?" Theologus scoffed. "In the Guidebook, the Sovereign One urges mortals, *Call to Me and I will answer you and tell you great and unsearchable things you do not know."*

"But by their very nature," I said, "mortals are materialists. They consist of material. Perhaps they cannot help themselves."

"You so quickly forget the words of Procrastin? That every mortal is endowed with the sixth sense by which may come awareness and implementation of the seventh? You recall the lineage of inquiry?"

I remembered the words of Procrastin, and I also remembered the words of the Guidebook.

> You will seek Me and find Me when you seek
> Me with all your heart.

"I am becoming aware of spiritual blessedness obtainable on Earth," I said, "and I cannot understand why so few partake of this blessedness. Would it not be wiser for the Sovereign One to bestow His fullness upon all?"

"This He has surely done!" exclaimed Theologus. "And He has enhanced His blessedness by making it available solely through choice!"

"Choice?"

"In bestowing the gift of choice, the Sovereign One gives to each mortal an essence of His own sovereignty. Were He to do otherwise, were His grace to be the natural birthright of all, mortals would become but spiritual automatons. Would you prefer to be a puppet guided by strings or a rational being with freedom to choose?"

"But because mortals may choose, must it be necessary for the Sovereign One to send some to a place of everlasting banishment?"

"The Sovereign One sends no mortal to such a place! Eternal banishment becomes one's destination only when eternal banishment becomes one's choice!"

Theologus had spoken with judicial sternness. His voice mellowed as he continued.

"I also experienced the turmoil which now troubles you. I could not understand the sinful nature of mortals and the supposed justice and mercy of the Sovereign One. When I had such thoughts, there was one word I could not bring my lips to utter."

"What was the word?" I asked.

"Hell," responded Theologus.

I collapsed, smitten by the distressing concept.

"As in my own case," I could hear Theologus saying, "the word rarely appeared in my vocabulary and never with credibility."

He took my hand, lifted me.

"You are not only troubled about fire and brimstone but by the origin of iniquity itself," he said.

"Yes," I struggled to say.

"If you are to fulfill your mission—"

"Tell me of my mission!" I interrupted with eagerness.

"Be patient." The voice of Theologus was both stern

and kind. "You must first be led into awareness, then into your awakening, which will identify your mission.

"Let me caution you. On Earth as in this domain, the Sovereign One welcomes honest questions of whatever subject or nature. But He also expects you to as honestly receive the answers to your inquiries. You must also remember that mortals must first be in awe of the Sovereign One before they can be in harmony with Him."

"Please explain."

"I came to the Sovereign One in early youth," Theologus continued. "This in itself benefits me here. However, I was endowed with unordinary intellect, or so I assumed. In my vanity, I thought how fortunate it was for the Sovereign One to have my services while others of my peers invested their minds in the pursuit of science and philosophy.

"I developed, as one mortal stated, an *I-it* relationship to the Sovereign One. I presumed to dissect His counsels, categorize His attributes, measure His grace. I was a fool!

"As you shall see illustrated in a subsequent encounter, the Sovereign One has made the basis for knowing Him simple, the experience of knowing Him profound."

"Is it wrong for mortals to pursue truth in itself?" I asked. "To investigate science, to evaluate history, to observe human conduct . . . ?"

"Not wrong," replied Theologus, "but, for many, dangerous. You know from your own experience, as do I from mine, how prone mortals are to infect their evaluation of truth with the taint of personal prejudice. I learned one cannot be curious about the Sovereign One and, at the same time, sincere in the search for Him. Attempting to comprehend or rationalize the Sovereign One, apart from the Guidebook, is to make the Sovereign One increasingly less comprehensible."

"Were you aware of the seventh sense?" I asked.

"Not until, in His mercy, the Sovereign One dealt with me much the same as He did with Procrastin.

"I was smitten by severe illness. Fear of death taunted me as though immortality, as Procrastin told you, were a state to be avoided. Through pain and debilitation, through the terror of death, I saw the emptiness of my mortality. I realized my finite intellect was retarded, when compared to the infinite mind of the Sovereign One. Rid of childish curiosities, driven by reverence and joy, my *I-it* mentality changed to *I-Thou* reverence and wonder!

"I confessed my pride, my pseudo self-sufficiency. My health was in measure restored. I became, in fact, more robust than I had been previously. With this gift of well-being, I entered a new relationship with the Sovereign One. I saw Him as above and beyond my mentality, as the Ultimate, the All in All, the First Cause, the Creator/Designer, Alpha and Omega, God very God and great I Am!"

The voice of Theologus had risen to resounding eloquence. Then, suddenly, he paused. He bowed his head, as though in prayer.

At last he continued in half-whisper, "I submitted to

Him, anticipated and awaited His guidance. No longer did I see the Guidebook as *containing* the words of God. The Guidebook became for me *the* Word of God!"

I recall Theologus having continued talking as he slowly disappeared from view. Then, like rain softly falling, came the words:

> As the heavens are higher than the earth, so are My ways higher than your ways and My thoughts than your thoughts.

Seven

I wished to question Theologus further as to the justice and the judgments of the Sovereign One.

But he was gone.

Or, perhaps, I had left him.

I no longer stood in the cathedral-like edifice but, instead, in a nondescript open area.

"It is for a purpose," I heard spoken from behind me.

Turning and looking about, however, I saw no one.

"You will find this place quite different from any other you have experienced."

Nor could I identify the voice.

"That is why we meet in a neutral setting."

"I . . . uh," I stammered, thinking some unintended deviation in my schedule to have occurred, "I am but in limited transcendence and . . ."

"Yes! Yes! I know! My circumstances are not all that different from your own!"

The bland surroundings began to take form and color, as though we were watching an invisible artist do primary sketching, then add dabs and brush strokes. The impression was at times surrealistic, as often abstract, even grotesque. Then, for a time, it appeared the artist chose to reshape the strokes and dabs into the preliminary shadings of a conventional work.

"What is the meaning?" I asked.

As though responding to my inquiry, the surrounding phenomena—in a manner similar to my experience with Algoris—became animated. Twisting, rising, falling, at times like breath, at times like pulse.

Until this moment, I had not observed that—but for the sound of my voice and the brief speaking of the person I had not yet seen—the visualization encompassing me had occurred in complete silence. Now, softly at first, I heard a variety of sounds: euphoria, gluttony, ecstasy, debauchery.

A frightening thing happened. The painting became dimensional, continuing to be animated but assuming substance as well as form until it was like a mad sculptor's statement in statuary. Metallic and plastic at first, adapting into thorny vegetation adorned with serpents, rodents, and what I assumed to be enlarged virus strains and, as it were, noxious bacteria.

"Why am I seeing this?" I cried out. "Where am I?"

A hand rested upon my shoulder. I turned and saw at last the person who had come to be with me.

"I am Sentium," said the new informant. "During my Earth tenure, as you likely surmise, I was not prone to having thoughts, not even on occasion, of immortality. Thus you do not see in me the attributes of a

Theologus, the intellectual manner of an Algoris or Astrophon, or even the characteristics of the commoner you observed in Procrastin. I am among those who achieved transcendence, by the mercy of the Sovereign One, at the moment of mortal demise."

"Deathbed," I said quietly.

"In my case lying along a roadside, fortunate to have one of your kind happen by."

I took closer observation of Sentium. He likely departed Earth in younger years. He had sensual bearings, yet was characterized by a childlike attitude, such as one would see in a young boy having his first look at a place of wonderment.

This attitude reflected in his voice as he said, "I am in multiples blessed to be here. How does the Guidebook state it—*a burning stick snatched from the fire?*"

"Where are we now?" I asked.

"Actually," Sentium replied, "we are yet in the open space where first you heard me speaking. The surroundings are but fabrication, a visualization of the subject we shall be considering."

"What is this subject?" I asked.

"False manifestations of the seventh sense," he replied.

The surrounding visualization now began to turn. Faster and faster, like a carousel. The whirling became a blur. From this mass of movement came a cacophony of sounds: garish laughter, brash shouting, drunken phrases, ecstatic screaming, obscene utterances lurid and profane.

How could this be, I pondered, in the sanctity of limited transcendence?

"Remember," reminded Sentium, "I told you what you see is fabrication."

"Are you in transcendence?"

"All praise to the mercy and goodness of the Sovereign One!"

"Please tell me. These manifestations . . . ?"

"The five primary senses gone awry," said Sentium, "the trauma and torment mortals encounter when they pander the five primary senses, and when the sum of reality is to them the sum of mortality."

I became increasingly confused.

"You will understand," Sentium assured me.

We now entered upon a most unusual setting, as though we had returned to Earth—or, I should say, a simulation of Earth. We walked upon streets and alongside buildings. Fine residences and, in our next stride, hovels. Prestigious edifices alongside ramshackle structures.

Men and women scurried about us. Some appeared to be tycoons, others entrepreneurs. Young and old. Male and female. The ladies, the gentry, those struggling for advantage, those whose countenances expressed frustration and unfulfillment, those who thought themselves in command of their destinies, those repressed, those baffled, and so many of them—so very many—darting about like wound up toys.

"They are searching where there is no finding!"

It was distinctly the voice of Sentium, spoken conversationally at my side, yet also as the mountain high proclamation of an oracle.

"So it was during my total mortality," Sentium continued. "Like those we see, I was ever seeking, never suspecting the object of my search."

"What was the object?" I asked.

"The seventh sense!" He spoke as though he presumed I already knew. He took my arm and turned our movement toward a doorway immediately beside us. "Come, let me illustrate."

We entered a large enclosure, ornately styled, filled with people and yet hushed to the verge of silence. Half sat at a long bar, as many at adjoining tables. The lighting was subdued, like illumination from candles, and yet I saw each face as separate and distinct. Occasionally one of those present lifted a glass to sip. A mood of tranquility pervaded the premises. To someone unfamiliar with the setting, it might be taken as a place of piety.

"This is a brotherhood," said a man at a table near us. He lifted his glass.

Another man at the same table lifted his glass and said, "A brotherhood."

Sentium touched my arm once more, and we were again on the street.

"Was it a brotherhood?" I asked.

"Fraternity, yes," replied Sentium, "brotherhood, no."

"Can there be true brotherhood apart from the seventh sense?"

"There cannot be."

We were presently under the marquee of a theater Women, scant-clothed in nonetheless stunning costumes, surrounded us. They embraced me. They kissed me and caressed me so intimately I struggled to break away, but instead, my feet moved, without an effort of my own, through an elaborate portico which brought us into a theater filled to near capacity.

The stage, half the size of the auditorium itself, thronged with men and women who, at first, appeared to be partially clothed. Their nude bodies had been painted, or perhaps tattooed, with lurid designs which accentuated the sensitive and sensuous features of mortal anatomy.

From somewhere in the building, an orchestra began to play. Not music one would suppose fitting for such a beholding but, to my considerable surprise, symphonic strains, melodic, soothing, rapturous. And, in time with the music, the performers on stage began the shocking pursuit of erotic ecstasies.

My heart pounded. My mind went awhirl. I was captivated, for—to my humiliation—I lustfully desired to be one of them.

The performers became gifted with levitation and came floating out upon the audience, continuing their exploits, looking down at their viewers, holding out their hands in the offering of themselves.

"Remember," cried Sentium, "they are searching where there is no finding!"

I was at once embarrassed and ashamed. I turned

from the spectacle, drawing an arm across my eyes. Whereupon the performers, suddenly all back on the stage, burst into such raucous laughter the building shook from reverberation.

Sentium took my hand. We were instantly gone from the theater, once more walking upon the street.

"They think they have found life's sublimest moment?" I asked, pointing back toward the theater.

Sentium did not respond but hastened our gait forward.

We became part of a living montage, which dissolved from setting to setting like a projected visual and yet, as I said, appeared to me as touchable reality.

"Fabrication?" I asked.

Sentium only smiled in response and gestured for my attention to a cluster of men. They stood stooped over a conference table. A set of large blueprints lay before them. Though somehow contained upon the table, these drafted plans spread out to the right and to the left as far as one could see.

I leaned forward, to better see the blueprints, but Sentium took my head in his hands and turned my eyes upon the men assembled. One of them walked to a facing wall, or I thought it to be a wall. He touched this wall, and it opened like a draped window. Before me, and before these men, spread a panorama of their craft—buildings of wondrous design, structures so tall their tops were veiled by clouds, or so wide each of them filled the full scope of the viewing area.

"The men!" Sentium exclaimed. "Observe the men!"

I looked at the men, but only for a moment, because the montage changed to the largest banquet hall I had ever beheld. The floor space was cluttered with tables, large and small, all bedecked with delicacies of innumerable variety and context. Men and women, in festive attire, dashed about from table to table, observing, sampling, imbibing.

"Faces!" shouted Sentium. "Observe their faces!"

I tried, but once more the montage changed location. Changed and changed. To clothing, comforts, instruments of pleasure, objects of affluence.

"Faces! Faces!" Sentium continued urging.

And I did take note of faces, although, at first, I could not discern the purpose of his urging.

But then I saw.

"Searching where there is no finding," I heard myself say.

Meaningless! Meaningless! I remembered from the Guidebook. *Everything is meaningless!*

"Is everything meaningless?" I demanded to know. "Is it?"

Again, Sentium gave no reply. Instead, a melange of faces passed before me; though living, they equally appeared dead. Young and old. The wealthy. The poor. All of them striving, searching. Faces and faces and faces.

"Searching where there is no finding!" I cried out, inquiry as much as statement. "They seek fulfillment but cannot find it!"

"Fulfillment can never be experienced in the five primary senses," said Sentium. "Do you understand?"

I did indeed!

"Those who seek mortal satisfaction—wealth, self-gratification, sensual ecstasy—can only do so in the primary senses," I declared. Then a thought came in illuminating brightness to my mind. "But when mortal acts are guided and enhanced by the seventh sense, then the primary senses respond with true fulfillment!"

"The highest function of mortal emotion," I heard Sentium say quietly, "is adoration of the Sovereign One!"

"And is the Sovereign One pleased when mortal acts involve the five senses hallowed by the seventh?"

I was once more alone, in the nondescript place where I had first stood before meeting Sentium.

And from the Guidebook, I heard:

> Never be lacking in zeal, but keep your spiritual fervor, serving the Lord.

 Eight

remember an expanse of vegetation, the abounding verdure one finds in a place well watered and carefully cultivated. I recall neither the green of growth nor the gold of harvest, however, as it was another of those instances where the meaning of a circumstance held my attention above its visual content.

"The meaning is simple!" a voice sang out.

I turned to see a pixie-like person bounding toward me in the manner of a child at play. Because of his adult features, I at first thought him a dwarf. As he came closer, however, I observed his stature as similar to my own.

Initially, his presence offended me, so strong was my regret at no longer conversing with informants like Algoris, Theologus, and Sentium. The newcomer's countenance and bearing—apart from his boyish actions—indicated a background far removed from lecture halls and research facilities. How ever could such as he prepare me for my mission?

"I am Fervence," said the newcomer. "I am simple. But not foolish. I was often called a fool, as was my father before me, but we were not fools. We were only simple. Do you understand? Not foolish. Simple."

Fervence began skipping and jumping, performing handsprings and pirouettes around me in a continuing circle of diminishing circumference.

As he encircled, he sang a tuneless ditty:

A simple soul am I.
This I cannot deny.
And simple you may well be, too.
But let us not chatter
Of things of no matter,
As so many are prone to do.

He repeated the lyrics several times, and I at first disdained the words, hearing them as trivia of an indigent culture. But with each repetition, the words penetrated more deeply into my thoughts, becoming surprisingly profound in their simplicity.

When the circle became so small he could no longer continue without brushing against me, Fervence quit his song and his antics, looked up at me, and said, "Isn't it wonderful? The plan of the Sovereign One is so simple I can understand." He stroked his chin in a moment of reflection. "But the plan of the Sovereign One is so meaningful, it wonders the wisest!"

He searched my face for response.

"I have ever been simple," he continued soberly.

Then, smiling, he added, "But my father taught me a man or a matter may be simple and yet meaningful. Do you understand? My father was a simple man. But meaningful. Oh, yes! Very, very meaningful! A simple man my father was, whose mind stood ever open to meaningful things. From his words and his doings, I also learned."

Spontaneously, he began once more to sing.

A simple soul am I.
This I cannot deny.
And simple you may well be, too.
But let us not chatter
Of things of no matter,
As so many are prone to do.

He had but sung the first few words when, to my astonishment, I joined him. Like choraliers, we sang. Like vocalists of finest repertoire, our voices blended in delightful harmony. I was by this time used to participating and, at the same time, listening as though removed from the point of rendition.

To my further perplexity, I desired instruction from Fervence as much as I had cherished the teachings of Theologus. The realization so overwhelmed me, I began weeping.

"Tears!" exclaimed Fervence. "My father taught me much about tears! 'Some of Earth's greatest meanings can only be spoken with tears,' he said. Do you understand?"

I raised my hand to dry my eyes.

"Oh no! You must continue weeping! Tears are a gift from the Sovereign One, my father told me. Isn't that meaningful? Simple but meaningful?"

I now fell into such an outburst of sobbing my emotions surged beyond control. I dropped to my knees. A rock-like substance was just beneath me, like an altar, and I cast myself upon it, my tears continuing until they furrowed the hard surface over which they flowed.

"Beautiful! Beautiful!" Fervence sang out. "See what your tears are doing!"

But I could not look.

For my tears were but the manifestation of a larger fountain within, the upthrust of a wellspring of contrition. I anguished over my dislike of simple things, of simple minds—my disdain for the assurances unsophisticates proclaimed, my amusement at their admonitions. I remembered how many times I had dismissed the whisper of truth, deep in my heart, to accommodate the view of some clever and heralded skeptic.

"O Sovereign One!" I cried out. "O Sovereign One!"

"Tears may also be prayers, my father taught me." Fervence seemed far away now, although I heard him distinctly. "Tears can bring much joy to the Sovereign One. My father taught me that. Isn't it wonderful? Wonderful and meaningful? To give joy to the Sovereign One!"

In that instant, the turbulence of previous moments gave way to a sublime calm. I felt renewed, to the marrow of my bones. I might have burst into song were it not for the healing beatitude the quietness brought to my thoughts.

"See now what your tears have done!" Fervence cried out.

I raised my head. The field surrounding us, of nondescript herbage when I first beheld it, had been transformed into a garden glorious. Flowers of ponderous size, together with blooms small as the rarest of gems, festooned the area.

"It was your tears! Your tears watered the plants and set free the blooms! Your tears did it! Your tears!"

If my tears released the blooms, then my joy discharged the fragrance. No previous aesthetics of limited transcendence surpassed the sheer elegance of that aroma.

"It is simple," said Fervence. "Your tears and the flowers and their smelling are a oneness. One! One! It is the most important number, my father taught me! Do you also understand?"

How singular, I thought, that the teachings of Algoris appeared comprehensible to this impaired person!

"As my father often said," he continued, "the more we understand meanings, the more we know there is but one meaning. Is it not beautiful? That is a thought the Sovereign One gave to my father. Only one meaning! Do you see?"

"One meaning," I replied, "beautiful."

For I saw my tears as subjugation, at long last, of my rebellious pride. And the blooms and the fragrance were one with my realization of having finally understood how futile is the finite, how meaningless Earth-centered passions and priorities, how abounding and impelling the infinite.

"It is simple," I said.

"Yes! Yes!" Fervence cried out in childish delight. "'Simple but meaningful,' as my father would say. 'We sometimes cannot know the meaning,' my father also said, 'but we can always know there *is* a meaning.' Isn't that meaningful, the words of my father?"

"Did you and your father know of the seven senses?" I asked.

"Not by the words but by the meaning. When I was a child, my father took me on long walks to places of beauty and quietness. He would sit for many hours, saying nothing. But saying much. Do you understand? He would point to a tree, touch a flower. In whatever he said, in whatever he did, he turned my thoughts to the Sovereign One."

I was witnessing the fruits of the unbroken lineage of inquiry!

"You asked questions of your father?" I said.

"Many!" Fervence replied.

"Your father answered your questions?"

"If he could. But many times, he said, 'You ask something your father does not know, my child.' I knew, when he spoke those words, he had spoken wisely!"

"But he did have answers to some of your questions?"

"'Your father is a man of small wisdom,' he would say, 'but wise enough to know we shall one day know as we are known. That is the only answer we are given

for many of our questions. We are fools to think otherwise.' Those were the words of my father. 'We are fools
to think the Sovereign One has forgotten to make an
answer to every question,' he said. 'Fools!'"

Fools!

Fervence could as well have spoken my name!

"My father came by my bed at night. 'I am a man of
common mind,' he often said, 'so I speak of things in a
common way. But listen, my child, listen to common
words which have meaning farther than we can hear and
higher than we can see and deeper than we can understand. *The LORD is my shepherd; I shall not want.* The
most simple of men can understand those words, but no
more meaningful words were ever written or spoken.'
Simple but meaningful. Do you see?"

"Your father taught you much about the Sovereign
One?" I asked.

"Oh yes! He spoke to the Sovereign One as to a long
and dear friend. He believed in the Sovereign One as a
baby believes in its mother. And in watching my father,
the Sovereign One became to me what He had been to
my father and to his father before him."

*One of the detriments of the mortal fall is the broken
lineage of inquiry,* I again remembered. And I also recalled
that *what is most to mortals is least to immortals.*

From distant horizons, and from deep within me,
came the words:

Anyone who will not receive the kingdom of
God like a little child will never enter it.

 Nine

Once more I stood alone.
Thoughts of Fervence occupied my mind, my prejudices about him having been so surprisingly subdued.

Yet I harbored a moment's disdain.

"He has had no difficulty believing in the fires of eternal judgment," I said aloud.

The words, spoken quietly from my lips, were picked up as by a wind and blown into an echo which grew ever louder until it shook the terrain upon which I stood.

I wanted to apologize for the utterance, to ask forgiveness, but could not speak further.

"For my thoughts are not your thoughts, neither are your ways my ways," declares the LORD. "As the heavens are higher than the earth, so are My ways higher than your ways and my thoughts than your thoughts."

"Who spoke those words?" I asked.

"I inserted them into the pattern of your thoughts." It was the Voice again. "You are disturbed, for you do not find answers to all your questions."

"I find many answers," I said, "and I am grateful."

"But with each answer, you are beset with more questions."

"And when I meet someone, and this transcended informant begins to relate to my learning—"

"—the informant is abruptly gone," interposed the Voice. "You do consistently remember that you are in limited transcendence?"

"But, also," I continued my complaint, "I am led into one terrain, often engrossed by the setting, and then suddenly I am ushered elsewhere."

"In your encounter with Fervence," asked the Voice, "did you not begin to escape from one of your most hindering weaknesses?"

"I did," I admitted.

"Then rejoice!" Now it was Theologus who spoke. "You must surely realize how singularly privileged you are."

I turned and, for an initial moment, thought my eyes beheld another stranger. Yet I realized the spokesman was indeed my former and most cherished of transcendent friends. It was as though we had not seen each other in a long interim, for there was a newness, a mellow and radiating humility, permeating his countenance.

"You first saw me as I was when I entered transcendence," he explained, "but now you see me as I more fully am."

"Do I also see you differently because of my larger awareness?"

"Reality enhances as awareness increases. Remember the words of Astrophon?"

"*One perceives that for which one is prepared,*" I recited. "Astrophon indicated a limitation to his perceptions here. Without the seventh sense in mortality, there is limitation in immortality?"

"*One perceives that for which one is prepared,*" Theologus repeated. He paused a long moment, then added, "You have become productively aware of the mortal brain and the immortal mind. It is assuredly true that biology and theology should be kindred studies."

"Especially true of the brain?" I asked.

"Not even in the misuse of their sexual organs do mortals so ignore the intended use of an Earth organism as in the misuse of the brain. As you know, the brain consists of two hemispheres—the left, which governs pragmatic functions and comprehensions of the Earth experience, and the right, wherein lie creativity, wisdom . . ."

I waited, then prompted, "And . . . ?"

"Sentium showed you false manifestations of the seventh sense."

"Licentiousness is a function of the brain's right hemisphere?" I asked.

"For some it is," said Theologus. "For most, licentiousness is but the further misuse of the five primary senses and becomes the most inferior of substitutes for what fools might suppose to be the seventh sense! Sentium also demonstrated for you how creativity, and the capacity for great exploits, can further deny mortals the joys of fulfillment through the seventh sense. There is marked similarity between the ancient pyramids and the edifices of your time on Earth!"

"Is the discovery and implementation of the seventh sense the primary purpose of the brain's right hemisphere?" I asked.

"The primary purpose of the entire mortal brain," replied Theologus, "is to contemplate and worship the Sovereign One!"

I stood once more in the heart of a void. I say "heart" because it was indeed such. Not an emptiness. But a rendezvous, where silence and the absence of distraction provided the mood for sublime contemplation.

The primary purpose of the mortal brain is to contemplate and worship the Sovereign One.

The words became a roundelay, whether audible or in thought I cannot say. Nor did I discern whether it was my imagination, or a viewed spectacle, whereby I seemed to be standing at a vantage point from which I observed the crafts of mortality. Artists fashioned paintings so realistic it was as though brush and hand created living scenes. These skillful ones put down their pallets, picked up musical instruments, and rendered symphonies of such content they would astound the most discriminating of Earth audiences. Abruptly, the musicians became architects, in moments designing and constructing buildings of spectacular form and size. And then, in the midst of their work, the architects became poets. Ignoring rhyme and meter, they composed snarling dirges of anger and despair. They cried out in eloquent blasphemy to the skies above them.

"O Sovereign One!" I exclaimed.

My words scarcely departed my lips when the montage was gone—swept asunder, it seemed, by my utterance.

Meaningless! Meaningless! Utterly meaningless!

"Take care not to misunderstand," I heard Theologus say, and realized he had not left my side during the interim. It was a comfort to know. "The craft of mortal hands is only meaningless when pursued without reference to the Sovereign One. You remember the admonition of the Guidebook: *Whether you eat or drink or whatever you do, do it all for the glory of God.*"

"Such has not been the case with me," I admitted with regret. When my friend remained silent a moment, I added, "But it shall be!"

Theologus took a step, as did I. We found ourselves in what I can best describe as the outskirts of a village. Before us stood pleasant little dwellings, resembling dollhouses in size but, also, in that they looked as though they had been constructed of many-colored sweetmeats and gingerbread. The streets were candied brick, each a different color, no two identical in hue or size or placement.

Theologus touched my arm. We stepped into the

village. The streets were empty. The dwellings appeared to be uninhabited. I turned to my friend, wondering. He gave a happy laugh, which was like a summons, for we were suddenly surrounded by chattering little beings so unique and delightful I could not at first identify them.

"Are they cherubs?" I asked.

Again my friend laughed, and said, "As near as one finds in this place! In actuality, they do not meet the specifications of Earth sentiments. They are, in some ways, the most fortunate of all transcendents, for they entered immortality in the aura of innocence."

"They are beautiful!" I exclaimed.

"And everlastingly happy," said Theologus.

"They comprehended the seventh sense?"

"No, but neither did they spurn nor neglect it."

I thought of children I had known, snatched from mortality in their infant years. The joy their lives had provided. The lingering sorrow. The empty places caused by their absence.

Away.

To this!

I watched, enthralled. The little ones before us joined hands and danced in the streets, leaping to the tops of their houses, on and on and higher and higher until they became as soaring birds.

During one interval, upon returning to their lovely habitat, they recited poetry. Sometimes in unison, sometimes in duet and trio, sometimes individually.

I remember a fragment of one poem.

*Children! Children! Let us be
Children for eternity!
Little children everywhere
Frolic in their Sovereign's care!*

One child bounded up to me, bowed and, like a prized pupil in an Earth recital, said, "It is normal for children to love and follow the Sovereign One. It is the fault of their elders that children do not always love and follow the Sovereign One."

He left as he had come, rejoining the others.

"One might better terminate mortality at birth?" I asked.

"Did you find the happiness of Fervence less joyful than the spirit of these you see here?" Theologus responded. "*One perceives that for which one is prepared.*"

I continued watching the creatures, in awe and silence.

A sobering thought beset my mind.

"Are these little ones better prepared for transcendence than those who departed mortality having made little or no preparation?" I asked. "Is it possible to be better prepared at birth than at death?"

Anyone who will not receive the kingdom of God like a little child will never enter it.

My mind went awhirl with questions, with postulates of my own.

"Can it be one must become as a little child," I asked, "because the mind of a child is closer to the wisdom of the Sovereign One than the mind of a sage who rejects or ignores the seventh sense?"

"You have spoken well," said Theologus.

"But I have become aware of concepts here which are farther beyond Earth wisdom than Andromeda is from Earth's sun."

Heaven is the infinite amplification of Earth's sublimest moment!

Before I could surmise whence the statement had come, whether spoken by the Voice or by Theologus or within my own thoughts, the little ones dancing and chattering about us were—like children, indeed—off to another whim.

I watched them go until my friend touched me for my attention, then pointed. Turning, I saw coming toward us what seemed at first a cloud borne rapidly upon the shoulders of the wind. I held up my arms, as one would protect himself from the impact of a sudden storm. Gently, Theologus restrained me and moved my arms downward.

Then I saw.

As the cloud came fully upon us, I realized it had not been a cloud at all but another vast company of little ones.

At first observance, their faces seemed identical. In coming nearer, however, I could see they were, most strikingly, individuals. Like snowflakes, like flower petals—identical in essence, diverse in detail.

"These departed mortality without having taken breath," Theologus said.

"They were denied breath?" I asked.

My friend did not reply. The etch of pain came deeply to his countenance. Simultaneously, the radiance of transcendent wisdom touched his eyes. It seemed he wished to smile but could not. He parted his lips, as if to speak, but remained silent.

"Had they not been denied the gift of life," I asked, "might there have been those wiser than Algoris, more perceptive than Astrophon, as devout as you, and . . . ?"

The ones of whom I spoke now came to me, surrounding me, singing, chattering, laughing.

"Earth multitudes," I gasped, "denied the fullness of their mother's wombs!" More quietly, I asked, "Had their progenitors permitted full gestation, might some of these have missed transcendence?"

Surely the wrath of man shall praise You.

Like thunder the words sounded! Like judicial pronouncement!

Did I detect a special bliss upon the faces of some of these wonderlings?

"Damned by their progenitors!" I exclaimed. "Redeemed by the Sovereign One!"

The little ones now rushed from me, as though frightened by my loud voicing, except that they continued singing and chattering and laughing. Above the din, I heard:

Where is the wise man? Where is the scholar?
Where is the philosopher of this age? Has not
God made foolish the wisdom of the world?

Ten

The wee ones, who had so fasci-
nated and distressed me, flew
beyond visible distance. Those whom I presumed to be
inhabitants of the village remained. They continued their
antics—chattering, rollicking, designing new games,
composing new songs, performing ever more compli-
cated choreography.

As I watched, I noticed those who, although they
participated with the others, differed in appearance and
movement. One little fellow particularly caught my
attention. He slipped, when prancing across a near
rooftop, and fell laughing a short distance from us.

"Is he injured?" I asked.

"Injury?" Theologus mused. "Here?" Then he
asked, "Would you like to meet Mongo?"

As though summoned by the mention of his name,
this Mongo of whom Theologus spoke bounded up from
his fall and came to me in one jump. Having at first
disdained Fervence, I should have detested Mongo. The
initial sight of him reminded me of Earth acquaintances,

a father and mother whose only child was born mentally impaired. Stunned and humiliated, fearful of the subsequent scrutiny of friends and family, they had the child committed to an institution.

It was plain to see that Mongo's mortality had been of similar circumstances.

"Praise Sovereign One! Praise! Praise! Praise!" Mongo exclaimed. He looked at me but spoke as though in prayer. "I Mongo! Mongo! Mongo! Know more than angel! Angel! Angel! Tell! Tell! Tell! Show! Show! Show!"

He came yet closer and I looked fully into his face. His countenance was one of bland simplicity, yet radiating with a glow of impelling alertness.

"You come! Come! Come!" he sang out. "See toy! Toy! Toy!"

As I indicated, my prior meeting with Fervence prepared me to accept Mongo as a celestial informant. Not that I fully accepted him. But neither could I reject him. For I knew divine purpose, surrounding each encounter, similarly engendered this.

So I offered my hand. Mongo took it and led me through the ornate portals of a structure beside which we had been standing.

Theologus accompanied us.

We entered an enclosure fully encompassed by a projection screen—above, beneath, all about.

"Seven! Seven! Seven!" Mongo exclaimed.

"You experienced dimensional audiovisuals on Earth." Theologus spoke with a lilt in his voice.

"3-D," I said.

"We think of Mongo's toy as 7-D!"

Mongo touched a control device. We were in that instant surrounded by such a crescendo of celestial melody, I held my hands to my ears. With the music came visuals, astounding beauty encompassing the whole of the projection screen, an Earth context unlike anything my own eyes had beheld upon the planet. There was a pristine aura and a fragrance like the musk of a baby's skin.

"Toy! Toy! Toy!" Mongo cried in delight. "Like? Like? Like?"

"What is it?" I managed to ask.

"Earth," replied Theologus, "at the time of creation."

"Simulation?"

"No, Earth as it truly was."

"But how?"

"Sunshine!" exclaimed Mongo. "Sunshine! Sunshine!"

"It is quite elementary," Theologus explained. "All the prior and present events of Earth are recorded in light reflected into space. Mongo's toy, as he calls it, can intercept reflected light at any point, however many light-years this reflection of Earth may have traveled from its point of origination. Doing so, Mongo can project any Earth event he wishes us to see."

"Can! Can! Can!" Mongo cried out gleefully.

Whereupon the little fellow activated his toy again

and again. As he did, events from Earth's past surrounded us.

I stood within primordial wonders, watched extinct creatures traverse long-fossilized forests.

"Like? Like? Like?" Mongo asked.

"Like!" I replied, unable to resist adding, "Like! Like!"

Now Mongo brought to the screen a montage of world events from the past. We watched Genghis Khan lead his golden horde to the shores of the Adriatic, witnessed Alexander's conquest of the known world, saw Charlemagne rout the pagan army across Saxony and Westphalia, and caught glimpses of the Corsican's ignominy at Waterloo.

"Mongo has become an avid student of history," Theologus said, as we continued watching, "although on Earth he could not have named the president of his country."

"But here . . . ?"

"The mortal brain," explained my friend, "even when encumbered as was the case with Mongo, possesses storage and response capabilities beyond that of Earth's most sophisticated computer. In his mortality, Mongo was better fitted for celestial perceptions than are most mortals whose minds are encumbered by neglect or rejection of the Sovereign One."

"Imprisoned within the five senses," I mused.

"Mongo's brief mortality was characterized by a strong motivation to learn," Theologus continued. "He did quite well in reading, struggled to cope with basic mathematics. He and Algoris have an endearing friendship."

"On Earth," I asked, "did he reach out to the Sovereign One?"

"Indeed!" replied Theologus heartily. "Had he been a normal child, his parents would likely have denied him spiritual encounters. They thought it no harm that Mongo was invited to children's First Day classes. He comprehended sufficiently to claim the love and grace of the Sovereign One!"

"See! See! See!" Mongo exclaimed.

"We must not ignore Mongo's performance," Theologus said. "He most enjoys scenes from the Guidebook."

"Yes! Yes! Yes!" exclaimed Mongo.

About us Guidebook events occurred in living dimensions. Crossing the Red Sea, which we saw three times at the little one's insistence; the falling walls of Jericho, which we viewed twice; the pomp and pageantry of kings; shepherd boy David minding his flocks and felling the giant; Ruth gleaning in the fields of Boaz; many more.

"Show us your favorite," Theologus suggested.

"Favorite! Favorite! Favorite!"

It was in the next moment as though we stood outside the City of Zion and had become numbered among the ancient throng.

"He comes!" someone cried.

"Comes! Comes! Comes!" Mongo echoed.

Out of the nearest city gate a procession emerged.

There were crying, cursing, clothing being rent, people trampled afoot, soldiers flailing their whips in unavailing efforts to subdue the mob.

A black-skinned man appeared, bearing a cross.

Beside him another Man.

"The Sovereign One!" I gasped.

Mongo skillfully manipulated the machine, so that the black man and the Man by his side filled the full of the expanse before us.

"Love! Love! Love!" Mongo sang.

It was electrifying!

"Black man love Sovereign One," Mongo said, speaking quietly now. "Sovereign One love black man."

"Yes!" I agreed. "Yes! Yes!"

"Mongo love Sovereign One," our projectionist added. "Love! Love! Love!"

We saw the full view again, as the procession ascended a hill.

"Crucify Him!" the people cried.

"No! No! No!" Mongo protested. Then, in a throaty outcry, he added, "Yes! Yes! Yes!"

On up the hill, to the very apex, went the black man and the Sovereign One. There two soldiers grasped the cross, spread it upon the ground, and thrust the Sovereign One onto it.

I wanted Him to defy them, to call down an army of angels!

I saw Him hold His hands into place. I saw the spikes driven in, slowly, mercilessly. I saw the cross lifted upright, dropped with a cruel thud into the prepared hole.

"*Eloi, Eloi, lama sabachthani!*"

"Oh!" I gasped. "The actual words? The voice?"

"Yes," said Theologus solemnly.

"Yes. Yes. Yes," affirmed Mongo, whispering.

The event came into sharper and more vivid detail as, everywhere about us, myriad faces began to appear, filling the screen, each obliterating the one it followed. Faces of the notorious, of the long forgotten, kings and princes, presidents and generals, men hailed as good, men decried as evil, faces, faces, faces, by the thousands, by the tens of thousands, by millions, billions, yet each distinct and identifiable.

"You see the face of every mortal," Theologus said.

"Of every mortal?" I asked.

"Every mortal."

"Of all time?"

"The Sovereign One bore the iniquity of all who had lived or who would live."

"*Father, forgive them!*" the Sovereign One cried. "*It is finished!*"

Opaque darkness came to the theater, so dense I felt myself wrapped in an imprisoning substance. Then, dimly but distinctly, in what I saw to be the first etching of morning dawn, a tomb lay before us. Sealed by a stone.

Outside the tomb, nether beings appeared. They were in celebration. Wherever I looked, I saw them—about, behind, above, below. They danced obscenely. They uttered profane renditions of damnation anthems. Closing my eyes caused the evil ones to appear the more distinct.

"O Sovereign One!" I cried.

"See!" I heard Mongo call out. "See! See!"

The scene remained for a moment unchanged. Then I heard distant thunder, coming closer and increasing in loudness until the sound took form in words from the Guidebook:

> I pray also that the eyes of your heart may be enlightened in order that you may know the hope to which He has called you, the riches of His glorious inheritance in the saints, and His incomparably great power for us who believe. That power is like the working of His mighty strength, which He exerted in Christ when He raised Him from the dead.

The thunder grew fully and incisively articulate. The words were repeated, becoming the very essence of power, so great the massive stone rolled away. The nefarious creatures fled, like soldiers put to rout, like cowards terrified.

A brilliant light filled the entrance.

Then silence.

Like angels singing, came the words:

> Christ died for our sins according to the Scrip-

tures. He was buried. He was raised on the third day according to the Scriptures.

I fell into a deep a trance. When I regained my senses, I was no longer in Mongo's theater but lying comfortably in a strange and quiet place.

"Where are we now?" I asked.

There being no response, I closed my eyes in contemplative repose.

 **Eleven**

I remember walking along a pleasant concourse. I remember touching. I remember succulent tastes, exotic aromas. Yet I cannot now give a description of my whereabouts at the time of these pleasures.

"You are doing well," I heard Theologus say. "You are adjusting to the primary condition of transcendence, in which the content of a place or experience is subsumed by the larger reality of awareness."

Awareness!

"Know, of course, that the word is not found in the vocabulary of transcendence," explained my friend, "but is here used to assist you in preparing for your mission."

"I have yet to learn of my mission," I protested.

"You will not need to be told." Theologus was a man of inherent kindness but not before had he spoken this to me with such gentility. "You will know what your mission is to be."

"And my one besetting question?"

"Concerning the fires of eternal judgment?"

"Yes."

"It would distress you, were I to tell you at this moment how that question, and its relevant aspects, will be laid to rest in your mind. In my own pursuit of the seventh sense, two counsels from the Guidebook helped me in this same matter. *We know and rely on the love God has for us. God is love.* Also, *will not the Judge of all the earth do right?* Remember the further counsels of the Guidebook, where we are cautioned to *see to it that no one takes you captive through hollow and deceptive philosophy, which depends on human tradition and the basic principles of this world rather than on Christ.* No mortal, having discovered the seventh sense, questions the acts or decrees of the Sovereign One."

"Can any word or concept enter mortal thinking in its correct meaning apart from relationship to immortality?" I asked.

"The purpose of mortal thought in the plan of the Sovereign One," replied Theologus, "is to provide a means of communication between the Sovereign One and those whom He created."

"May I never again look casually at a flower!" I affirmed. "Or the sky at night! Never relate space/time and the material world inwardly rather than outward and upward!"

"You are discovering the high priority of submitting yourself to the workmanship of the Sovereign One!" My friend paused a long moment, then added, "You have come near to the time when you will set at rest your most perplexing question."

"The eternal damnation of those unrepentant?" I asked bluntly.

Rapport between us had grown to such measure I felt the freedom, if not the ease, to speak with such frankness. How wise, I reasoned, his spending so much preparatory time for whatever it was he would tell me.

"I am unable to understand," I began, eager to hear what my friend would say, "why the Sovereign One has not made transcendence the natural lot for all mortals."

"Awareness is the obedient daughter of revelation, rationalization the errant son of reason," said Theologus.

"It is wrong to reason?" I asked in considerable surprise.

"Remember the words of the Guidebook? *'Come now, let us reason together,' says the LORD.* In the Sovereign One's plan, revelation validates reason. Mortals err in assuming reason validates or invalidates revelation."

From the Guidebook:

> I will destroy the wisdom of the wise; the intelligence of the intelligent I will frustrate.

"It is characteristic of mortality to resist belief and embrace doubt. By an act of His will, the Sovereign One chose to create. By an act of the will, the created may choose to embrace, resist, or ignore the Sovereign One.

You must understand the wisdom and grace of being given the right to choose!"

"Choice enhances the joys of transcendence?" I asked.

"Were it not for choice," responded my friend, "there could be no transcendence. In choice, the Sovereign One put within the reach of every mortal fulfillment and bliss angels can never know!"

"Fervence and Mongo—" I began.

Theologus interrupted to say, "Fervence and Mongo were chosen for your visit to intensify your awareness and to underscore a most important point; namely, what one perceives in transcendence, and thus enjoys as fulfillment, depends directly upon the sincerity and intensity of Earth-time preparation."

"So that," I asked, "those like Procrastin, who could have arrived much better prepared, do experience fulfillment in transcendence? But it is with the tempering knowledge that, had they as mortals on Earth made the choice to more properly prepare themselves, their perceptions could be much more fulfilling?"

"Your use of Earth reasoning is inadequate for assessment here but necessary to the carrying out of your mission. In that sense, you are provisionally correct."

Quietly, in distinct articulation, came to my thoughts the words of the Guidebook:

> The Spirit searches all things, even the deep
> things of God. For who among men knows
> the thoughts of a man except the man's spirit

within him? In the same way no one knows
the thoughts of God except the Spirit of God.
We have not received the spirit of the world
but the Spirit who is from God, that we may
understand what God has freely given us.

"The seventh sense!" I exclaimed.

"Discovering and implementing the seventh sense as
a mortal on Earth," Theologus explained, "is the first
stage to abundant fulfillment in transcendence. Com-
parison and self-seeking, however, are as alien to the
seventh sense as are greed and lust alien to holiness."

"Fervence and Mongo then," I continued, "do not
attain the measure of fulfillment Procrastin might have
known—"

"There are no such encumbrances as the measure of
fulfillment," Theologus said. "Were you in full transcendence, you would encounter the company of those who
have, by their own choice, come to this place. Yet you
would not think of comparing your lot to theirs or any
of them to each other."

"If fulfillment is the same for everyone," I asked,
"and if one is not aware of the greater or lesser fulfillment experienced by others, then what is the incentive
for mortal preparation?"

"Again you resort to Earth logic and measurements,"
Theologus scolded, "both of which are unrelated to
experience here. Have you so soon forgotten the princi-
ple? *One perceives that for which one is prepared!*"

"But you just said—"

"To compare one's lot with others is one thing," Theologus interrupted, "to perceive within one's self is another! Earth preparation is a matter of choice, enhanced in the seventh sense between each individual mortal and the Sovereign One."

"Does the joy of fulfillment then relate to a knowledge of how sincerely and earnestly one has prepared during mortality?"

"One perceives that for which one is prepared."

It occurred to me I had become so enrapt with our subject, I had set aside my concern for the grim alternatives to transcendence.

"Is it of no matter here," I asked, "the fires of judgment?"

"One of the great joys of my transcendence is to know that I have been redeemed, and that, by choice, I took unto myself the merits of redemption. But choice is an option of mortality alone.

"Those who by choice selected contrary options, are left to the wisdom of the Sovereign One. We need not question the lot of such."

I raised my hand in momentary futility.

"No need to lament or protest!" insisted Theologus. "I am in the realm of eternal bliss by choice. As may you be also. For choice is the greatest gift the Sovereign One could bestow upon mortals, except for the greater gift of His everlasting love and redemption."

I felt ashamed, penitent, and said, "Then I ought not to ask concerning sin and judgment?"

"To the contrary! Your question need not go unanswered, though its answer is foreign to the inquiry and dialogue of those in full transcendence. The answer will be of value to you in your forthcoming mission, and you shall have it. I only caution you that it has taken until this point in your limited transcendence for you to accept the means whereby you shall have your questions put to rest."

"Please explain!" I urged.

But I was again alone, and there came upon me another of those sensations by which I knew I had entered a most holy state. I sensed, and correctly so, this state to be the prelude for an experience which would underscore for me a promise from the Guidebook which had, on occasion, perplexed me:

> Now we see but a poor reflection as in a mirror; then we shall see face to face. Now I know in part; then I shall know fully, even as I am fully known.

Twelve

I know! I know! I know!"

Mongo appeared at my side. He placed his arms lovingly about me. A moment's warmth touched my heart, then a breath of resentment. I had been promised an answer to my questions about sin and eternal punishment. Surely this menial transcendent could not help me, when profound Theologus refrained!

Why not Astrophon or Algoris?

Or even Sentium?

"I know! I know! I know!" Mongo repeated insistently.

"What do you know?" I asked.

Mongo loosed his embrace. With both hands, he took one of mine and led me forward. We were presently inside his projection facility.

"Seventh dimension?" I chided.

"So! So! So!"

I laughed, as one would laugh at a pleasantry injected

into conversation alluding to the admitted weakness of another.

Mongo also laughed.

I sensed warmth in his laughter. And love. It was like a song. Joyful. But I also realized that, whereas I had laughed in a way somewhat demeaning of him, it was he who now laughed pitying me.

Overt displeasure arose in my heart, an emotion so alien to the temperament of my celestial experience my cheeks went hot with embarrassment. Yet I could not bring myself to apologize. How ever could this impaired child assuage my lifelong fretfulness about passages in the Guidebook concerning eternal damnation?

Mongo saw my altered disposition.

Small though he was, the lad became like a towering giant in that moment. He swept me into his arms, holding me without effort. He looked down upon me as does a compassionate father to his injured or fearful son.

I remembered the words of the Sovereign One: *Anyone who will not receive the kingdom of God like a little child will never enter it.* I remembered the Apostle's counsel: *God chose the foolish things of the world to shame the wise.*

"You know Bible!" Mongo ventured cautiously. "Know! Know!"

He began to laugh. I laughed with him, in this case laughing as do friends in a circumstance mutually enjoyed.

He put me down, and I stood beside him once again, our girth and stature as they had formerly been, except that size became insignificant in such a moment. We threw our arms about each other in hilarious camaraderie.

"Sovereign One!" I cried loudly. "This boy has more knowledge of You than the sum of all my Earth knowledge! Let him teach me! Make me his willing pupil!"

"Oh!" Mongo gasped, startled. "Oh! Oh!"

"It is the truth of my heart," I said to him. "If the Sovereign One would speak to me through you, then I will listen as though it were He talking to me!"

My prior resistance fell like loosed shackles from my soul, and I waited in eagerness for what the boy would tell me.

"Now!" he exclaimed. "Now! Now!"

He bounded away to the contraption in the center of his cinema, activated the control lever as he had previously done. We were in the instant surrounded by a dense woodland, a carpet of moss and leaves beneath, wisps of sky above.

"The Sovereign One made all these trees, didn't He, Father?"

It was the younger but unmistakably distinct voice of Fervence! Was I to be further demeaned by condescension to both Mongo and Fervence for the response to my prolonged and painful inquiries?

"O Sovereign One," I whispered, and forbade any further manifestation of my Earth vanity and prejudice.

Like a frantic child, I ran toward the woods—so realistic was the projection—and might have thrust myself against a portion of the screen had not Mongo bounded after me and intercepted my trajectory. We fell, the two of us, to the forest's floor, except it was a hard surface with only the visualization of moss and leaves. My little friend said nothing but, silently, rested my head in his lap as he looked down at me with wide, wondering eyes.

"Yes, my son. The Sovereign One made every tree, every branch, every leaf. The Sovereign One made them all."

I sat up and looked away and saw Fervence, in his younger years, exploring the woods with his father. The two bore distinct resemblance, in stature and countenance, in the intellect I had so disdained. They stood just above me, and I reached to touch Fervence in greeting but my hand only passed through his projected image.

The father stooped and picked up two branches, holding one in his right hand, the other in his left.

"From what kind of tree has each branch fallen?" Fervence asked.

"The Sovereign One knows," replied the parent. "I am in wonder of all He has made and done. But I am also a man of little knowledge." He sighed. "Such a simple mind is mine, not to know the names of the trees the Sovereign One has placed in tne forest. Even though I may one day have been told, I have by this day forgotten."

He tossed away the branches in a gesture of sadness. He stood a moment beside his son, then walked to one nearby tree and picked up a seed, walked to an adjacent tree to gather another. These he held in each hand for his son to come and see.

"They look alike," the father said, "but each will grow a different tree. It is because the Sovereign One has placed instructions in every seed. Plant these seeds anywhere in the forest, and one will grow into one kind of tree," he pointed to the tree at their left, "and the other will grow like this," he said, pointing to the tree on their right. "The seeds will grow as instructed. They have no ability to choose otherwise."

Fervence reached for the seeds, restrained himself.

"You wish to plant them?"

"May I, Father?"

"I would be pleased. The Sovereign One would also be pleased."

Fervence took the seeds, looked about, and saw an open space to which he scampered. There, in frolicking excitement, he planted the first seed. He saw another open space to which he proceeded with continuing zest and planted the second.

"Two great trees will one day grow where you have this day chosen to plant their seeds," said the father. "You chose. The seeds could not choose."

"Perhaps the biggest and perhaps the most beautiful trees in all of the forest," said Fervence.

"Perhaps, my son."

The two walked on. I stood, remaining in my place and yet following them.

"So very small, the seeds," I heard Fervence say. "So

very big, the trees. It is because all seeds obey the Sovereign One."

"So can it be with us, my child. We are very simple. But we can choose to obey, as do the seeds. The Guidebook tells us Earth's least can become Heaven's most. But only if we choose and if we obey."

A brook gently flowing now appeared. The two sat beside it.

"It pleases the Sovereign One when the seeds obey Him," said Fervence.

"Yes," agreed the father, "but, as I have said, the seeds have no choice. It pleases the Sovereign One much more when you and I obey Him, for you and I could choose not to obey."

The two sat unspeaking. I waited, my expectation as keen as had been my anticipation for the words of Theologus and the others.

"I choose to obey the Sovereign One," said Fervence at last. "I choose always to obey Him." With delight, he added, "So I am like one of the seeds!"

"You are more than the seeds!" There was the hue of reproof in the parent's voice. "You can obey or you can choose not to obey. That makes you greatly different."

"What is it to obey, Father?"

"It is to look into the pages of the Guidebook and learn and follow the instructions."

"Just as the seed obeys instructions?"

"Yes, but much more. To be a person is much more

than to be a tree! As I told you, a person may choose. A tree may not choose."

Fervence looked up and about him and said, "I would like to be a tree, Father, but not unless I could also be a person." He continued looking at the trees and added, "The trees are very beautiful."

"And think of our eyes, my son, given to us by the Sovereign One so we can see the trees. And our minds, so we can know the trees are beautiful. And our lips, so we can praise the Sovereign One for giving us such beautiful things. In all the world, nothing is so beautiful and meaningful as to praise the Sovereign One."

"I praise Him, Father. It was you who taught me."

"It was the Sovereign One who taught you. He only used my lips."

The two quietly studied the flowing water. I watched, intent. Not even the words of Theologus had so caught my attention or heightened my anticipation.

"There is so much to know about the Sovereign One," the father said at last. "The wisest of men is as a child in the first days of learning."

"Is it too much to learn?"

"The very much we cannot know about the Sovereign One," replied the father, "is meant to help us more surely know Him!"

"Your words are higher than my ears," Fervence said.

"Higher also than mine. But not higher than our hearts!"

The two stood and continued walking into the forest.

Fervence scooped up a handful of seeds. He studied them as the two walked.

"Seeds have no eyes, no ears, no hands or feet, yet they obey the Sovereign One."

"Spoken wisely, my son! Do you see that the Sovereign One has made knowing Him and obeying Him simple enough for the mind of a child? Any mortal, however simple, however lowly, may know and obey the Sovereign One."

There came now a loud roaring. The two turned to look, as did I. A short distance from us, a large area of the forest had become engulfed in violent, destroying fire.

"Can we put it out?" the boy exclaimed.

"No, my son," replied the father quietly.

"Why must the trees burn? Did they disobey the Sovereign One?"

"Trees can only obey. They know not how to disobey."

"Then why must they burn? I would not burn them, if it were mine to choose!"

The man took the hand of his son. They walked in silence. They walked far. They ascended a hill and walked down into a valley.

"I am glad we have gone away from the fire," said Fervence. "I could no longer bear to see the trees burning."

The father gave no reply. Instead, having reached a second vantage, he pointed. Before them lay a large area of the forest where, long before, the trees had been razed to their roots by fire. Here, however, the forest had begun to regrow. Saplings and flowering plants, green and rainbow-hued and fragrant, arose in healing from the earth. Only on an occasional here or there could charred remains of the previous conflagration be seen.

"There is much teaching for us to learn from what our eyes now see," said the father. "I pray the Sovereign One will grant me the wisdom and the words to share the teaching with you."

"One day the Sovereign One let the fire burn," said Fervence, "and it made a great ugliness. Now the Sovereign One grows new trees and plants, and it is beautiful. Was the fire a goodness?"

The father picked up a fragment of scarred timber. He held it beside a sapling green and strong.

"What does the forest teach us?" asked Fervence.

The lineage of inquiry! The words came to my thoughts with renewed relevance.

> Every child born on Earth has the curiosity
> necessary to inquire about the Sovereign One
> and His doings.

"I cannot tell you why the Sovereign One permits beautiful trees to burn," said the father, "but my mind is full of wonder and my heart is full of praise to see new things growing where once there were but ashes and sadness."

"Fire makes many trees die before they are old."

"And death will come to us, my son. Death is our fire.

So if we have only lived for what is now, death's fire will leave us nothing but ashes. You do not understand my words. But remember them, dear Fervence, and as you grow older, you will understand."

"I will remember."

The two came to a fallen tree.

"This tree did not burn," said Fervence, "but it fell."

"We can see the reason for its falling," said the father. He pointed to the rotted center of the trunk. "Even while it stood tall and proud in the forest, this tree was dying from hidden rot."

"Like disobedience in the heart of a person, Father?"

"Like disobedience in the heart of a person, Fervence."

The lineage of inquiry!

"I am a simple man," said the father, after prolonged silence. "Others think thoughts and speak words beyond my mind and tongue. But I, like you, have wondered about the fires in the forests. I have wondered about the falling of tall and beautiful trees." He became quiet again, before adding, "I have wondered about wrong."

"Why is there wrong?" the young one asked. "Did the Sovereign One make evil the same as He made fire and death?"

"Evil was not of the Sovereign One's making," replied the father.

Fervence waited for his father to continue.

I also waited.

Anxiously.

"I was much older than you before such thoughts and questions entered my mind," the father began. "Perhaps you will not be so simple a man as I have been. But let me warn you, my dear Fervence. If, as you grow older, your thoughts and understandings are less simple than mine, be sure your thoughts and understandings are not less meaningful."

"I wish always to have such thoughts and words as the Sovereign One gives to you," said Fervence.

They sat quietly once more.

Then the boy asked, "Why is it some choose to love and obey the Sovereign One and some do not?"

There was again silence.

My anticipation increased.

"A word I have learned but do not understand," the father said, "is the word *infinite*."

Fervence formed his lips to repeat the word, could not, and asked, "What is the meaning?"

"The word *infinite* can only be spoken of the Sovereign One," the father replied. "For the Sovereign One to be *infinite*, it means He is greater than all He has made or will ever make or could ever make. Do you remember what our shepherd said one First Day about the stars and the planets? Do you remember the words he read from the Guidebook?"

Fervence stood, thoughtfully pondering, before he said, "I remember the meaning but not the words."

"The Guidebook tells us the Sovereign One sits on a high throne. The Guidebook says the Sovereign One *stoops down to look on the heavens and the earth*. He stoops to look down at all He has made because He is greater than all He has made! Our shepherd said the Sovereign One can hold all the stars and all the planets in his hand as a child holds small stones! Do you remember?"

"I remember!" the boy responded with enthusiasm.

"This is because the Sovereign One is *infinite*. Also, *infinite* means the Sovereign One has always been and will always be. The word has many more meanings, more than my mind can know or my lips can speak."

Fervence gathered a few stones and held them in his hand.

"What is the greatest lesson you have learned about the Sovereign One?" the father asked.

Fervence dropped the stones and stood like a schoolboy reciting. "The greatest lesson I have learned about the Sovereign One," he said, "is that He loves me."

"Well-learned and well-spoken!"

"Does He love the trees and the birds and the animals, Father? Does He love the stars and the planets?"

"Oh yes, my son! That is why the Sovereign One made the stars and the planets, so He could love them!"

"Is that why He made you and me?"

"It is, my son! It is! The Sovereign One made the stars and the planets. He made the mountains and the trees, the birds and the animals. Then He made people. He made them to enjoy the stars and the planets. He made them to enjoy our earth and the flowers and trees. But, mostly, the Sovereign One made people so they could

wonder about the greatness of His doings and the goodness of His doing them."

Wide-eyed, the boy waited for his father to continue.
With as much eagerness so also did I!

"As we know, only the Sovereign One can be infinite.
For Him to make anything, it must be less than He is.
And anything less than the infinite Sovereign One could
not be fully perfect as He is fully perfect. Also, for people
to truly love the Sovereign One, they must be able to
choose to love Him or . . ."

The father hesitated.

". . . or choose not to love Him," the boy said softly.

"What would it mean to the Sovereign One for us to
love Him, unless our love was by our choice?"

"Is choosing not to love the Sovereign One the greatest of all wrongs?" Fervence asked.

"It is, my son."

"Would it have been better for the Sovereign One not
to make us?"

"Wiser tongues than mine have spoken that question," said the father.

"I would not wish to have been unmade," the boy
observed thoughtfully, "but that is because I choose to
love the Sovereign One."

"Long before He made people," the Father continued, "the Sovereign One made a plan. He planned a
wonderful gift, which could only have meaning if you
and I could accept the gift or refuse it. He made this plan
before He made the stars and the planets!"

"What was this plan, Father?"

"You have heard it since you first came to my knee. You learned how the Sovereign One Himself came to Earth, born as a baby."

"I know! I know!" Fervence cried out.

"In the great plan, the Sovereign One became our Redeemer before He became our Maker."

The boy's countenance grew troubled. The father laid his hand lightly upon his son's shoulder.

"What is it?" the father asked.

"If we did not choose to love the Sovereign One," inquired the boy, "what would happen to us?"

"As you said, the greatest of all wrongs is to choose not to love the Sovereign One. The Sovereign One chose to make us and to love us. But for those who choose not to love Him, the Sovereign One has no choice. He must send them to the place where evil is kept separated from good. Do you understand?"

"I understand," replied the boy.

"You understand the Sovereign One could have chosen not to make us and not to love us?"

"Oh!" exclaimed the boy. "That would have been very sad!"

"And it is very sad when a parent or a child chooses not to love Him. The sadness in the Sovereign One's heart hurts Him much more than the fire hurts the forest. Do you understand?"

"Yes, my father, I understand."

"Do you also understand that the Sovereign One could not bring us to His place of everlasting joy and wonder unless we permitted Him to prepare us for that place?"

"If such mortals came to that place," exclaimed Fervence, "then it would no longer be a place of joy and wonder!"

"Spoken wisely and spoken well, my son!"

Fervence looked away.

"I am troubled," he said.

The father waited. Fervence turned back to him.

"Some of those we know and love do not know and love the Sovereign One. When we go to the place of joy and wonder, and when those we know and love do not come with us . . ."

The boy began to weep.

The father waited.

At last Fervence looked up and asked, "Will we see them? Will we watch as we watched the fire in the forest?"

"The Sovereign One makes no mistakes. His plan is good and wise. His place of joy and wonder will give no room to sadness or badness. We leave it at that, my son. We leave it at that."

Taking the boy's hand, the father led him further into the forest until they were gone from my sight. A wind arose, gentle but strong. The wind rustled the leaves. The wind moved the branches toward each other and away from each other. And the wind became a voice, which sonorously intoned:

> Whoever believes in the Son has eternal life,
> but whoever rejects the Son will not see life,
> for God's wrath remains on him.

Thirteen

nly through freedom of choice could the Sovereign One bestow upon mortals the grace and love which motivated Him to create them!"

The voice of Theologus brought yet another phenomenon upon me. My total mortality—each action, each deliberation, each choice from my farthest memory to that present moment—was fully remembered. All thoughts, desires, motives, and experiences paraded through my mind, and the whole of it in one overwhelming moment.

What a poverty-stricken adherent of the Sovereign One I had been!

"Life is a farce," I cried at the full of my breath, "unless it is linked to eternity!"

Wood, hay or straw came in reverberating echo from the pages of the Guidebook.

Before I had time to feel judged or condemned, however, a second scenario paraded similarly before me the whole of my experiences in limited transcendence—

the events my eyes had beheld, the thoughts my mind had pondered, the alterations in my Earth-prone assessments.

How blessed I was and how privileged!

"You are experiencing a foretaste, although but a morsel, of the Sovereign One's grace and forgiveness," explained Theologus.

"*Heaven is the infinite amplification of Earth's sublimest moment!*" I exclaimed.

An eventide of repose came over me, of longer duration than the quiescence I had experienced prior to meeting Procrastin. In the first moments, I thought I could have remained forever in such utter bliss and tranquility. Indeed, there was a sense of endlessness to the occurrence, although I distinctly recall its beginning and its termination. And yet this perception of bliss had a distinct aftertaste, like a sweet draught laced with bitterness.

"If you were in full transcendence," I heard my friend say, "even though ill-prepared as many of us found ourselves to be, what you have until now experienced would be whimsy compared to the reality by which you would find yourself surrounded and endued."

"In limited transcendence one could not bear the joy of such reality?" I asked.

"Assuredly not!" came the reply.

"What is the measure of my present awareness in limited transcendence as compared to the comprehensions of full transcendence?"

"Again you err," Theologus chided pleasantly, "endeavoring to calculate the infinite with the measurements of the finite!"

What is most to mortals is least to immortals, I remembered from the counsels of Algoris. And, from Astrophon, *One perceives that for which one is prepared.*

"I am truly repentant," I said.

"And as truly mortal," added Theologus.

He touched my arm to proceed. I held back. He turned inquiringly but also with a compassion new to his pleasant countenance.

"Prior to meeting Procrastin," I said, "I experienced what I first supposed to be total bliss."

"Total but not fulfilling?"

"Yes."

"Knowledge comes to all who would know," said Theologus.

Before I could respond, we came to what struck me as familiar surroundings, although I could not identify the location or, in fact, feel any need to so do.

"We must be sure your mind is at peace concerning your Earth questions," Theologus introduced. "You have become fully aware of the seven senses."

"I have."

"But you hold reservations concerning the mortal right of choice?"

"I learned much from the simple ones," I said, "both the father and his son."

"From their counsel, you understand that the Sovereign One did not create evil," Theologus continued.

"The Sovereign One only permits evil, as the inevitable result of choice."

"The Sovereign One controls evil?" I asked.

"Controls and subdues it," replied Theologus, "and uses it to grant mercies and bestow blessings mortals could not know in a state of innocence. Evil is a mortal option but, through adherence to the counsels of the Guidebook, in no manner a mortal inevitability."

"What of judgment?"

"The wrath of the Sovereign One and the love of the Sovereign One are identical. For the Sovereign One's wrath is only against evil and the Sovereign One's judgment falls mercifully upon those who invoke it by spurning or ignoring the counsels and provisions of the Guidebook."

"Judgment a mercy?" I asked, perplexed.

"Ah, yes! A mercy to unredeemed and unprepared mortals for whom a moment of transcendence would be worse than an aeon of perdition! The purpose of mortality is not only to emerge at death into the bliss of transcendence, and thus escape the pall of judgment; the purpose of mortality is to exercise the five primary senses in the enjoyment of the Sovereign One through the perceptions and enrichments provided by the seventh sense. '*I have come that they might have life, and have it to the full*,' declares the Sovereign One."

"And so," I inquired, "does preparation for transcendence provide the greatest happiness in mortality? The most productive use of the five senses? The five senses enriched by the sixth and seventh?"

"Your awareness delights the Sovereign One!"

"But the awareness I have experienced here could as surely be experienced on Earth?"

"Two aspects of awareness you must take with you, as you leave to pursue your mission. First, during your Earth tenure, you have censured the Sovereign One for providing, in His mercy, the fires of judgment. In so doing, you have neglected to recognize the measure of your own iniquity. You have failed to see that the sum of your own righteousness is like *filthy rags*, the best of you falling utterly short of the Sovereign One's standard. You would have better spent your time seeking and pondering His mercy, realizing the ache of His heart toward lostness infinitely exceeded your own. For of His passion, the Guidebook informs you, *'He is patient with you, not wanting anyone to perish, but everyone to come to repentance.'* The most lamentable of all mortal weakness is to be ignorant of or insensitive to lostness and spiritual debility.

"The second awareness you must cherish and explore is that, as you have already been informed, you will find in the Guidebook and through the implementation of your seven senses, all and more of the concepts you have discovered in limited transcendence. Earth fulfillment occurs only through the seventh sense, as Procrastin informed you, in the joy of preparation for transcendence."

I fell to my knees in contrition. Theologus reached down and drew me abruptly to my feet again.

"You understand my words?"

"I do!" I exclaimed. "And I am more eager to experience on Earth what you have said than I am for any further glories I might behold in this exalted place!"

In that moment, Theologus was gone. Nor did I see him again, him or any other informant.

Fourteen

Mightier than the forces in Earth and space, substance in excess to ocean deeps and mountain heights, the girth of suns and the weight of planets—superlative to all was the exercise of the Sovereign One's mind and might in the generation of choice. The choice He made in creating entities and beings lesser than Himself. The endowment of mortals with the right to favor or flout His preferences, to decree their own everlasting destinies, to receive or repudiate unmerited rights to His unlimited favors."

In the moment, I presumed Theologus had returned and spoken. In the next moment, I realized the utterance came from my own lips. Yet not my lips at all but, in the manner of prior communication, the words were conceptual—ever more eloquent in essence than in articulation.

Nor stood I in any of the prior locations, or a place relevant. I was lying, eyes closed. But not sleeping. I had the feeling of arrival, as when one returns from a long and purposeful journey. I extended my arms, felt texture in my surroundings. It was a bed. And there was the pungent odor of pharmaceuticals, a mumbling of voices.

I opened my eyes.

Startled at the surroundings, I attempted to sit up. A woman's hands restrained me, a woman dressed in what at first appeared to be transcendent apparel.

"There, now," she said quietly, like a mother soothing her child, "it is good you are awake but you need much rest. Quiet yourself and rest."

I lay back, refreshed as if after a full and good sleep. In the distance, a hospital page could be heard. Calling for a doctor. Promptly. To emergency.

Emergency?

So it had been, in my case!

"O Sovereign One!" I uttered softly.

"What is it?" the woman at my bedside asked.

I did not respond, only smiled.

"You are doing well," she said. "You need not be apprehensive."

The woman stood another moment, then turned and left the room. I glanced at the table beside my pillow. On the table lay a copy of the Guidebook, which I eagerly took and opened to read.

The woman returned.

"Now! Now!" she chided pleasantly. "I told you there is no need to be apprehensive!" She glanced at the Guidebook, reached and took it from me. "You aren't going to die!"

"Oh yes I am," I replied quietly, "so I must first prepare to live!"

She looked at me curiously. She placed the Guidebook back onto the table. She gently fluffed my pillow. I closed my eyes in contemplation.

"Rest," the woman said. "That's it. Get all the rest you can."

I heard her footsteps, out of the room and into the hallway. I placed my hand upon the Guidebook but did not, in that moment, take it again.

Through my thoughts ran the words:

The Sixth sense.
The Seventh.
Heaven is the infinite amplification of Earth's sublimest moment!

Turning to the window, I saw people passing on the adjoining street. Mortals. Such as I had been. Unprepared, the likely lot of them!

I looked at the Guidebook.

I looked out onto the street.

With anticipation and delight, I proceeded to contemplate and to calculate my mission!

Scripture References

Throughout this book, Scripture references were used in the context of conversation between characters. Since this is not a nonfiction work, it is not appropriate to place the references in the text. For your information the references and the pages on which each one appears are listed.

Page	Scripture
8	1 Corinthians 2:10-12
11	Hebrews 4:9
15	1 Corinthians 6:19
17	Psalm 37:4
17	Jeremiah 29:13
17	1 Corinthians 10:31
19	1 Corinthians 2:9
24	Matthew 7:14
25	James 1:5
25	Matthew 6:31-33
25	Proverbs 3:5, 6
27	Jeremiah 15:16
27	Psalm 119:105
27	Psalm 32:8
27	Joshua 1:8
29	1 Corinthians 3:11-13
30	James 4:14
36	Psalm 147:4, 5
38	Psalm 19:1
39	1 Corinthians 2:9
41	1 Corinthians 2:9
45	1 Corinthians 3:12
	Psalm 139:17

46	Mark 8:36
50	Ecclesiastes 1:2 (KJV)
52	Psalm 8:3, 4
57	2 Peter 3:8
59	Psalm 90:2
64	Jeremiah 33:3
65	Jeremiah 29:13
69	Isaiah 55:9
75	Zechariah 3:2
80	Ecclesiastes 12:8
81	Romans 12:11
91	Psalm 23:1 (KJV)
92	Luke 18:17
95	Isaiah 55:8, 9
99	Ecclesiastes 1:2
	1 Corinthians 10:31
101	Mark 10:15
103	Psalm 76:10 (NKJV)
103	1 Corinthians 1:20
113	Matthew 27:46
113	Luke 23:34
	John 19:30
114	Ephesians 1:18-20
114	1 Corinthians 15:3, 4 (paraphrased)
120	1 John 4:16
	Genesis 18:25
120	Colossians 2:8
121	Isaiah 1:18
	1 Corinthians 1:19
122	1 Corinthians 2:10-12
125	1 Corinthians 13:12 (paraphrased)
130	Luke 18:17
	1 Corinthians 1:27
139	Psalm 113:6
143	John 3:36
147	1 Corinthians 3:12
150	John 10:10 (paraphrased)
151	Isaiah 64:6
	2 Peter 3:9

About the Author

Ken Anderson founded Gospel Films, Inc., an organization that produces Christian movies for worldwide distribution, in 1949. In 1989, he founded InterComm, a ministry that uses audiovisual media to evangelize the world.

Ken has published several books and is a frequent contributor to magazines and periodicals. He and his wife make their home in Warsaw, Indiana.